JACKAL IN THE GARDEN

An Encounter with Bihzad

D E B O R A H   E L L I S

WATSON-GUPTILL PUBLICATIONS/NEW YORK

Series Editor: Jacqueline Ching
Editor: Laaren Brown

First published in 2006 in the United States by Watson-Guptill Publications,
a division of VNU Business Media, Inc.,
770 Broadway, New York, NY 10003
www.watsonguptill.com

Library of Congress Cataloging-in-Publication Data
Ellis, Deborah, 1960–
Jackal in the garden : an encounter with Bihzad / by Deborah Ellis.
p. cm.
ISBN-13: 978-0-8230-0415-7
ISBN-10: 0-8230-0415-5
1. Bihzad, 16th cent.—Juvenile fiction.
[1. Bihzad, 16th cent.—Fiction. 2. People with disabilities—Fiction.
3. Nomads—Fiction. 4. Artists—Fiction. 5. Afghanistan—Fiction.]
I. Title.
PZ7.R25475Jac 2006
[Fic]—dc22

2006012444

This book was set in Stempel Garamond.

Printed in the U.S.A.
First printing, 2006
1 2 3 4 5 6 7 8 9 / 14 13 12 11 10 09 08 07 06

To those whose art and words
have disappeared through folly.

"We possess only what will not be lost in a shipwreck."

EL GAZALI

Preface

Kamal al-Din Bihzad was born into a world of turmoil and expansion. All around him, nations were shifting, empires were crashing and rising, and new ideas were springing forth like green shoots after a rainstorm. A growth in trade was expanding people's horizons and economies, and the Islamic world was celebrating a golden age.

In the great cities of Baghdad, Constantinople, Cairo, and Damascus, some of the most magnificent libraries the world has ever seen were being built. Rulers respected and funded artists and scientists, creating gathering places where talents and information could be shared and furthered.

As in the European world, it was a time when science and superstition clashed as never before, with reason poking holes in religion and vastly different ways of interpreting existence battled for ascendancy.

Bihzad lived a life quite apart from this turmoil, yet still affected by it. Into the library where he lived came the great thinkers and artists of his time. As old rulers collapsed and were replaced by new ones, Bihzad had to struggle with the place in the world of the elite he had been granted by virtue of his talent and circumstance.

Persia perfected the art of the book. Calligraphy was considered the highest of all arts because it gave humanity a tool for reading and spreading the words of the Prophet Muhammad. The illustrations in these books were paintings in miniature, and considered essential to the telling of the story.

Because of the Islamic law forbidding making lifelike images, Bihzad and the other artists had to take great care not to violate this rule. Many of the works of Mani, an artist who predated Bihzad by a thousand years, were destroyed after Mesopotamia (the area we now call Iraq) was conquered by Muslims in the seventh century. It was not until the Mongols overthrew the Islamic caliphate in 1258 that the rule was relaxed and images such as Bihzad's could once again be created.

Bihzad's work is among the greatest of all Persian treasures, and shows us a society of enlightenment, of beauty, and of deep appreciation for all the possibilities of this world and beyond.

CHAPTER ONE

I was born to die.

Born into a harem of beautiful faces, mine was twisted and misshapen, a lump of clay crushed beneath the foot of an elephant. A dark red blotch stained my features, like wine spilled upon my skin.

Wine should be in a cup, not on a girl's face.

Born into a household of strong, supple bodies, mine was lumpy and unbalanced, causing my mother so much pain she passed out during my time in her passageway.

"The child is cursed," the midwife said, holding me up to the Master. "Her birth was a mistake."

"She is of no value," the Master, my father, declared. I was a girl, and an ugly girl, worth no more consideration than a donkey too lame to work.

His disregard came to mean nothing to me.

"Put her to the jackals," the Master said. His word was law. My mother, unconscious from the pain and strain of delivering my misshapen body, could not protest.

A manservant took me in his arms and carried me out of the compound, through the streets of Mashad, and into the desert.

The manservant did not have to journey far from the city to find the desolate place that would be my cradle and my grave. I was told he laid me gently on the rocky ground. I was also told he gave me a kiss on my tiny cheek. I don't believe this. Why kiss something so ugly? Why kiss something you are abandoning to die?

The patch of ground where I was left was on the top of a bare hill, close to the sun and the moon. There I stayed, for three days and three nights.

My mother recovered from her childbed fever. This is a rare thing for women to do, and caused the servants to begin their whispers about the spirits. Mama reached for me. She saw heads hang. She saw eyes look away.

"Where is my child?" she asked. "It was not a dead-birth. I heard it cry before I went dark. Tell me now—where is it?"

They still didn't answer.

"Was it a girl?" Mama asked. "Was there something wrong with her?"

My mother knew the practice. Hers was not the first child of the harem to be put to the jackals.

"The Master ordered it," the other wives said.

"And you raised your voices in protest, I am sure." Mama looked especially hard at Shalia, the wife whose third child had been taken to the desert, but not until my mother's rage put gouges in four servants. She got away with such temper because she was my father's first wife, and short of committing treason or adultery, she was accorded his protection. No one could kill her but him.

Shalia avoided my mother's eyes. "The child was not right," she said.

"A girl, then," said my mother. "The child was a girl, and she was alive."

"She was a mistake."

"No child who manages to get itself born alive is a mistake." My mother went after the manservant. "Take me to her."

"But the…It's been three days!" He did not want to mention the jackals, for fear of angering my mother further, but everyone knew. A full-grown man alone in the desert would have to struggle to stay alive. A baby was instant food for many things.

"There may be something left of her to bury," my mother said. "I would like a grave to visit, and a memory to honor."

The manservant still wasn't convinced. My mother's request was not unreasonable, but it was not in keeping with my father's wishes. The servant had no moral objections to disobeying the Master. He just did not want to suffer for it.

Finally, my mother convinced him by reminding him that, as first wife, she had more power than he did, and he could therefore blame her if they were caught.

They left the protection of the compound under the further protection of the nighttime. They went out into the desert and climbed the hill where I had been left.

I was still alive.

"The moon shone a ray of light right down onto you," my mother told me, many times over the years. "You looked up at us and smiled."

The manservant was terrified. "An infant with power over the desert," he declared. "Powerful jinn."

"Powerful infant," my mother said, refusing to give the spirits any credit for my survival. She picked me up—the manservant cowering—and cradled me in her arms through the desert and the city streets.

"She can't stay here," the other women said, after they got over the shock of seeing me alive. "She should be dead. She will be a curse on all of us."

"She is a baby," my mother said. "She will be a blessing."

"She is a monster."

"She is a little girl."

"She is an ugly little girl. She will be an ugly woman. She will have no worth."

"I'll give her worth," my mother said.

"The Master doesn't want her."

"*I* want her," my mother stated, with unshakable firmness. "She is staying."

There was a long silence, then Farima spoke. She was the youngest of the wives at that time, and the one most often bothered by my father. She said, "We will have to keep the child a secret."

Who doesn't like to keep a secret from the Master? The one who owns us, who thinks he controls our lives, our thoughts, our souls—who doesn't want to keep a secret from such a person? Even my great ugliness did not take away from the pleasure the idea of a secret gave to the women in our enclosed world.

"What if he should find out?" Calima, the second wife, asked. She had more to lose. She didn't have the respect of the first wife nor the current appeal of the last.

"We don't need to actually lie," the latest wife said. "How often does he ask us, 'Is there a child among you who should not be there?' Never. We just need to be silent. The Master likes his women silent. And his servants," she said, looking severely in the manservant's direction.

The manservant had no plans to talk. He had obeyed his orders, had carried me out to the place of death. That I had not died was not his fault.

"Let's take another look at her," the youngest wife said.

The youngest wife was smart, just like my mother. She knew that you can't catch ugliness by being kind to an ugly person. Ugliness does not leap from one person to another. It stays by itself, hard and lonely. The youngest wife stood by my mother and looked into my face.

"Her face will become beautiful to us," she said.

"Her face is already beautiful to me," my mother told them. I was suckling. The worst part of my face would have been hidden against her bosom.

"She will need a strong name," my mother said, "a name that will make her brave."

She called me Anubis, the jackal, the Egyptian god of the dead, "for she has shown power over death."

Legends followed the name.

"The jackals encircled her at night and kept her warm with their breath."

"The vultures spread their wings during the day to shield her from the sun."

The stories spread among the household staff and, as legends do, they grew with the telling.

My mother fed me these legends with every drop of milk. As I got older, I knew they were just stories. Why would jackals warm me but not eat me? Why would vultures go against their nature and keep me from turning into their supper?

And yet, I had survived, defenseless, in a place designed to kill.

Something had kept me alive.

And for some reason.

We choose what we believe. I chose to believe my mother.

I chose to believe that I was special. And that I didn't need anybody else to tell me that.

Both beliefs would save my life.

CHAPTER TWO

For the first twelve years of my life, I lived encircled in the protected world of women, children, and legends.

The others agreed to keep my mother's secret because she was the senior wife, and because they loved her.

She was the first wife, and barely sixteen years old when my father married her. He was not an important man yet. That would come when his father died and he killed his older brother. He hungered for power, though, and showed his appetite for it in his treatment of his servants and my mother.

My father's mother, my grandmother, was a woman of great strength. I never met her, but stories went around the enclosure. She knew her son. Sometimes a mother will let her love for her child make the child's flaws invisible to her. But my grandmother knew her son. She knew him as she knew his father, and she protected my mother.

There was only so much she could do, of course. Her reach extended only so far, and she did not encourage familiarity. The notion of her exchanging confidences with a woman so low in status as my mother was at that time absurd. My mother found her cold, but dependable.

"She never treated me with cruelty," my mother said, and the other women in the harem concurred. "I could not go to her with my sorrow. She expected correct behavior from me, and she did nothing to alleviate my loneliness. But she knew her son, and made no excuses for him. We were united in that truth. We did not speak it, but I could see it in her eyes. She loved her son, but she did not like him."

My grandmother spared my mother whenever possible. She could not interfere in my parents' bedroom, or stop my father from using his fists and his feet, but she could and did send my father on trips for the family's benefit. She appealed to his vanity. "No one can judge those horses as well as you," or "Who else can command that battle? Only you."

Maybe she was hoping her son would take a spear in the chest. Things happen on battlefields, some of them lucky.

These trips gave my mother a holiday. For two weeks, even months at a time, she could sleep through the night, birth her children in peace, and let her wounds heal.

My mother produced girls, all born dead, except for me. My father tolerated this for as long as his purse made it necessary, then got himself another wife.

Women who love their husbands must find it rough when he brings another woman into their home. I heard stories from the later wives who remember growing up with fights in the harem. Some women would attack other women or tell lies to make them look bad. It's a practice that makes no sense. Why attack someone who is on your side?

There were no such quarrels in our house. Who could love my father? There were tears of pain, of homesickness, even of laughter, but not of jealousy. A new wife meant the old wives had a better chance of sleeping through the entire night. A new wife was someone to be embraced, not shunned. We all became healers, and looked after one another.

Our world was small and protected. The wives were fed and pampered by servants, and had few duties beyond the bedroom. We found things to do and things to laugh at.

My mother came from parents who praised Allah by educating His creatures. My mother and her sisters could read and write. They were well versed in astronomy, mathematics, and the arts. My mother was the smartest of them. It's a crime she had to marry my father.

Sometimes serpents can appear first as sheep. By the time their fangs start to show, they are half buried in your leg.

My father seemed like the ideal suitor. He said the right things, paid the right respects.

"He didn't marry me with the thought of beating me," my mother said, by way of explaining, not excusing.

Does it matter? What are intentions? Useless.

Intentions allow us to lie to ourselves and to others with a clear conscience. Intentions allow us to pretend we are better than we are. Action is the only truth.

You are surprised to read such philosophy from a monster like me? That is because you are a fool. You still think that monsters look monstrous. Why haven't you learned yet that monsters can have pleasant faces and voices so calm you become entranced by their evil?

People like me are easy to avoid. If we come too close, toss a few stones and we scurry away like rats, back into the shadows. When people like me approach you, we are looking for affection. We are not looking to destroy you. We are not after your soul, just your companionship.

My first years were happy.

As an outcast daughter of a wife no longer summoned, I posed no threat to the standing of the other children. My ugliness was almost appealing when I was a toddler—even baby hyenas are adorable, even baby warthogs—and I thrived on the doting of many bored women. I was smart, cheerful, and as helpful as my deformities would allow, so I became a favorite of the servants. They were used to being abused or, at best, ignored.

"Always say 'please' and 'thank you,' and greet them by name," my mother said. That's what she did, and I followed her example. "Slaves and servants are human beings whose luck has run out. They are no different than we are."

Sometimes I would watch my mother press against the walls of the enclosure, as if the pressure of her fingertips could push the walls away. She knew herself to be a slave. She also knew herself to be a human being, and, like all human beings, she would have preferred to gaze upon the horizon than to stare at a wall.

My mother built up my sense of importance, whispering secrets and legends to me in the dark. She spent most of her time training me. The poems of the great Rumi were my lullabies. I ate geometry with breakfast, played chess in the afternoon in the shade of the cypress tree, and read all the books in the household. She got the servants to teach me to cook and clean and look after the livestock.

"Will my brain have enough room for all these things?" I asked once.

"Your brain is just getting started," my mother replied. "You could learn new things every day for a thousand years and still have room for more." Then she quoted Rumi to me: "'You must prepare yourself for the time to come in which there will be none of the things you are used to.'"

Anything my mother thought might be useful to me, she went after, mental and physical.

My twisted shape would never let me be graceful like the other children, who pranced and twirled like butterflies.

"But there is no excuse for weakness," Mama said. She created exercises to make the most of the muscles the great Allah gave me. When she learned that one of the guards was an expert in sword fighting, she exchanged her favors with him for lessons for me.

Take that judgment from your eyes. We use what currency we have. My mother put her head on the chopping block every time she bought me a new lesson. Was there ever a braver woman?

"What will my future be?" I asked her on my thirteenth birthday.

I knew I was too ugly to marry, and by then the life of the enclosure was getting too small for me anyway. At night, when I could, I would slip out of the women's place and explore the shadows around the house. I had spent nights in the desert. In my dreams I could still taste the possibility in the cold night air.

My mother brushed my hair until it was as soft as fleece. She kissed my wine-stained face and touched scent from a jar to my temples.

"You will have the gift and the curse of making your own future," she said, holding me close.

I breathed in her flowery scent. I would have been content to spend the rest of my life in her embrace.

CHAPTER THREE

Changes started to happen in our little world.

A new wife came in, one who did not yet understand the exquisite pleasure of hiding things from the Master.

And I was no longer a cute little baby hyena. I was a full-grown wart hog. My brain and my mouth had grown along with my muscles. I was no longer a pet. I was an annoyance.

"Why are you teaching her poetry?" this new wife asked my mother. "Teach her to clean the latrines. That's all a creature like that is fit for."

My mother started to reply calmly that cleaning the latrines was as noble a job as any other, but I interrupted her with the suggestion that this new wife clean out the latrine with her ugly hairdo. I learned the sting of the new wife's hand as my mouth replied before my common sense could hold it back.

"I rejoice in my ugliness," I declared to everyone one day, with regal haughtiness. "By my ugliness, I will be remembered. Beautiful people are everywhere. You get tired of looking at them. After a while you all look alike. But someone who is truly ugly is indeed a sight to behold."

I impressed myself with this speech, but no one else.

"The world is not kind to ugly people," my mother whispered to me that night. "To do what you will have to do in this life, you will have to learn wisdom."

"Can you teach me wisdom?"

"No. You will have to learn it for yourself. We all do."

I was still for a while then, listening to the cries of the night animals in the desert.

"Mama," I asked, "what is it that I will have to do?"

"I don't know" was her reply.

The next twelve months brought many more slaps to my deformed face as my search for wisdom tried the patience of all the wives, new and old.

Their patience was also tried by the Master. A downturn in his fortunes brought out a side in him that was even uglier than me. He had always been a brute, but his old meanness was like a hobby. His new meanness was a vocation. Wives would return in the morning from his bed with bruises and bloody clothes.

The more evidence I saw of his brutality, the happier I was that I had been born ugly. I would never have to marry.

For years he had not called for my mother. He was mostly finished with her by the time I was a toddler, and she had enjoyed a long time of peace. But now he remembered her and began to call for her regularly.

I didn't like being abandoned. The new wife would taunt me and give me orders to clean up after her, as though I were a servant. My status was even lower than a servant's, but my pride was the pride of a sultan. The other wives grew weary of our arguments. I hadn't realized what a buffer my mother was until she was no longer there.

My troubles paled, though, when my mother started returning from her husband battered and bloody like the other wives. Her senior status was no longer a protection.

I tended to her wounds, the way she had tended to those of the other women.

One morning she did not return. He kept her with him for three days and three nights, the same length of time I had been in the desert.

Two manservants carried her back to me.

She did not recover. She passed away in the dark. At least I was with her.

I did not cry out or awaken the others. I performed in silence the dignities to her body.

In silence, alone, I gathered up my things. Into a sack went the cast-off garments of servants and others in which I had been clothed. I had little else to my name.

I took the sash from my mother's robe and wound it around myself. Her embrace would always be with me.

I gave my mother's battered face one final kiss, then left the women's place. There was no need to say good-bye. They would all be relieved that I was gone.

I knew my way around my father's house. In the kitchen I found dates and olives, bread and dried fruit. I packed what I could and slung a goatskin of water over my shoulder.

I didn't stop to plan. I didn't think about anything. I moved as if my movements had been preordained, as if all the events of my life had been building to this point.

Perhaps they had been.

I went into my father's bedchamber. He was alone on the bed, flat on his back. Snoring. He had all his limbs, and his face was uncursed by the ugliness that cursed mine. A healthy body, squandered on meanness.

This was my father lying on the bed, sleeping off his fine meal. From the day I was born, he had nothing to do with me, other than sentencing me to death. I was nothing to him.

And now he had killed my mother.

Now he was nothing to me.

I put down my bundle and the goatskin of water.

My father's sword was on the floor, casually dropped in the way that the arrogant and vain do because they cannot imagine they have enemies.

I picked it up.

I was awkward, but strong, and the sword-fighting lessons had helped me to not be afraid of the weapon. I used both hands. I plunged the sword into his chest. I felt it break bones in his rib cage, tear through flesh, and divide his wasted heart.

He stopped snoring.

He did not cry out.

He did open his eyes, just at the final moment of death. I hope he saw me clearly. I hope he recognized in my monstrous features the monster that he was himself.

He died quickly.

To this day I wish I could kill him again. I wish I could revive him, introduce myself as the flesh of his flesh and blood of his blood, then plunge the sword once more into his body.

That is my only regret. I feel nothing else, no guilt, no remorse. I have felt more compassion for the scorpions I crush after shaking them from my shoes.

I pulled the sword out of my father's body and wiped his blood off on the bedcovers. I tucked the sword into my mother's sash, picked up my bundle, and reslung my goatskin.

I walked through the house and out of the compound. There was no reason to look back.

I am Anubis, the jackal, the god of the dead. As I walked through the quiet streets of the city at night, I could feel the desert of my dreams call to me.

I knew it would protect me.

I was not afraid.

CHAPTER FOUR

It was not long before I discovered that the desert of my dreams and legends was not the desert of the wide-awake world.

"With all that space, why are people crowded together in cities?" I used to ask my mother. I kept wondering, long after she had ceased answering my question.

Before that first night was over, I knew.

They crowd together for comfort, out of the hope that if the Unknown attacks, it will take someone else, and not them.

I was all alone. If the Unknown wanted a victim, there was no one else to point to.

My muscles were hard from the exercises my mother made me do, but I still found myself straining to move through the sand, up the dunes, and down the other side.

As I moved, I kept listening for a cry from the city, outrage at the discovery of the murder of my father, the thunder of horses as men with swords rushed out through the city gates after me. There was no such commotion. If my father's death was discovered that night, the finder kept silent about it.

I moved away as fast as I could, straight into the desert, away from the city. Part of me was tempted to go back. The roars of the night hunters, the cold of the ground without the sun, the vastness of the sky frightened me as it would any mortal. I was plagued with remorse at not giving my mother a proper burial. I had chosen vengeance above honor, but was that the right choice? Were they the same choice?

The debate that raged in my mind was greater than my fear and propelled my legs forward in that dark night. With each step I took, I was damned further. Not for the murder of my father—of course I was damned for that, but it was a damnation I bore willingly—but for the lack of respect I had paid to my mother's body. What sort of daughter was I?

I panted hard up a rocky hill, bumping into bushes, scratching my face on brambles. At the top of the hill, I made a decision. I would turn and go back, bury my mother properly, and be executed by whoever cared enough about my father to soil his sword with my blood to avenge his death.

(Who would avenge *my* death? No one. The cycle of executions would end there. Probably a good thing.)

Sweating and breathing hard into the cold air, I turned around.

The city was nowhere in sight.

No glow in the sky from lanterns or cook fires, no sounds from fights or from lust. The desert was dark and empty.

"The desert is a place without beginning and without end," one of the legends in the enclosure went. "It swallows up men and armies and the breath of whole civilizations."

I knew this legend wasn't true, because I had met people who had crossed the desert. Some merchants came from across the sea. Some guests came from lands across mountains and deserts. Their wives would come into the enclosure. Once they got used to my ugliness, they would tell me of their lands and customs, their journeys and their childhoods. I learned their languages. Once they knew I was safe, that their secrets would remain locked within me, they all talked. Women have a lot to say.

I knew that the desert had an end and a beginning, and that people roamed it and lived off it, and that whole generations made their homes there.

And I knew, looking out at the dark land and the speckled sky, that I had just become one of those people.

There was no turning back. My disrespect to my mother after her death would become part of the burden that I carried on my humped and twisted back. It was right that I should feel its weight.

******

I kept moving that night. Movement warmed me, and I was too troubled to rest. All through the heat of the next day, I moved as well, my steps slower and shorter, moving only to avoid being set upon by the vultures that circled above.

"You're supposed to shield me from the sun with your wings," I cried out. If only legends were true.

They kept circling for a while, then flew off in another direction. I was thankful to whatever had just died and called them away.

I walked all that day and all of the next night. I mourned my mother as I walked, reciting prayers for her soul. I thought of her on her journey to heaven. By walking through the desert, I felt as though I were on that journey with her.

I stopped walking when the sun came up the next day. I took shelter under a rock ledge, brushing away the scorpions, checking for snakes. When I awoke, the sun was already starting to go down.

I drank sparingly from the goatskin and ate a few dates. Luckily, grief dulled my appetite. I started walking again.

For days, this was my life.

A few hours into the tenth night, I began to hear music.

Was I mad? That was a good possibility. I'd seen people go mad, servants, wives of guest husbands. People escape into madness when their reality is too harsh.

(My mother took good care of all the wives of my father. None went mad under her watch.)

I stopped walking and listened. The sky was rumbling with a desert storm, but I heard it again, the sound of music and the laughter of men.

I climbed up the next ridge. When I reached the top, I went down on my belly. The darkness protected me as I peered over the crest.

Down below me, a group of men sat around a fire. One of them strummed a long-necked instrument, making a lovely sound. From their strange assortment of clothes, I knew they were bandits. Castaways from their tribes, they had found one another and had formed a new tribe.

I watched them undiscovered from my ridge, breathing in the smell of the roasting meat from the spit over their campfire. I planned to wait until they were all asleep, then creep into their camp and take what I could.

After a while, amid much laughter, one of the men got up and went into the goatskin tent. I heard screams, and I knew they had stolen a woman.

Each scream brought more laughter. The man playing the instrument made the music dance, a sick accompaniment to their prisoner's fear and agony.

My mother would have rushed into the valley then and there, swinging her weapon and making them pay. She would not have weighed the risk and the outcome. She had a fierce courage.

I was not my mother. I waited. When they were asleep, I would steal their food *and* set their captive free.

They passed the wine around, getting louder and more vile, then quieter, until the only sounds that came from them were snores.

Arrogant fools! They were so certain of their own brutality, they hadn't even posted a sentry.

I slid down the hill on my belly, just another serpent among the night creatures. The precautions were unnecessary. The bandits didn't wake up.

I stole food and water first, wrapping the remains of the roasted animal in a sack I found on the ground. I took only what I could eat or drink or use to keep warm. It would have been foolish to take any of the jewelry they'd stolen. Not knowing where it came from, I could end up trying to sell it to its original owners.

With the food and water hidden over the hill, I went back for the woman in the tent. I was careful to cover my face as I ducked down under the goatskins.

She was already dead. They had used her, then cut her throat.

I went back outside. I was damned anyway. How many eternities could I spend in hell?

I went from man to man. I raised my father's sword and brought it down on their throats. Heads rolled away from bodies. The buzzards would feast well in the morning.

When I got to the last man, I raised my sword again, then stopped.

Anybody could leave dead bodies in the desert.

I was Anubis, the Underworld Child, the girl who didn't really exist, the girl who was protected by jackals and buzzards. I was not just anybody.

I bound the hands and feet of the man who still lived, then bound all of him to one of his beheaded companions. He woke up just as I was tying the final knot.

"What? Who?" As consciousness pushed its way into his wine-soaked brain, I let the cloth fall from my face. I enjoyed his screams.

"I am Anubis," I said, my foot on his shaking body. "I was left to die in the desert, but the buzzards and jackals saved me. Remember me the next time you think about hurting a woman."

I gave him a kick, then walked out of the little valley and gathered up the stash of food.

I thought about waiting around until morning, to watch his face as the full horror of the night hit him with the first rays of the sun, but his screams disturbed my thoughts.

I shouldered the food and walked on. A few hills later, and I was again wrapped in silence. The desert had swallowed up the sins of the night.

The sun rose. I slept well.

CHAPTER FIVE

Not all my enemies would be drunk and asleep. My father's sword was my friend when there was no opposition, but I wielded it clumsily, despite the lessons. I practiced with my shadow when I awoke in the evenings. My body had strength but no grace.

My ugliness would protect me to a degree, but I couldn't depend on it for everything. I would have that moment when my enemy first saw my face and recoiled, and in that instant I could slip away. But men who do ugly deeds are used to ugliness in all its forms. They live with it in their minds and would not be repelled for long by my monstrous features.

The desert was not empty enough. I would need an edge.

I found one.

The meat from the bandit's campfire—I think it was goat—sustained me for several days. I awoke one night thinking I should gorge myself on the rest, before it went rancid. I unwrapped it, to feast before I began walking again. I'd leave the bones instead of carrying them. The desert would pick them clean.

I heard a sound then, a sort of yelping. I looked around but didn't see anything. The sound repeated and came closer. It was a small sound and didn't scare me, but I wanted to know what it was.

Out from beneath the rock that shaded me from the sun came a baby jackal. It was alone. It moved on three legs, awkward, like me. I guessed it couldn't keep up with the pack and had been abandoned. Also like me. It was a scrawny creature, all eyes and appetite.

I tore a piece of meat off the carcass with my fingers and held it out to him. He didn't want to take it from me.

"If you want to eat, you'll have to do it my way," I said softly. "We can help each other, but you'll have to trust me."

His hunger outweighed his fear. He came closer, sniffed at the food, then grabbed it quickly. In an instant it was gone. He sniffed the ground, looking for more.

A jackal is a dog of the underworld. It is said to be in league with the devil, to be feared and mistrusted.

My mother had named me after a jackal to give me strength, and to make my enemies wonder.

"We are alike," I whispered, holding out another morsel of food, this time a little closer to my body.

It looked at my face, as if wanting to know if I was serious about making him come so close. He didn't recoil at my features.

"You don't know that I'm ugly, do you?" I asked, keeping my voice low and gentle. "You're nervous because you've never seen a human before, but you're not disturbed by the horror of my face."

Here was a creature who would like me if I fed it, and would trust me if I didn't beat it. It didn't care that I was shunned, something that should never have been born, a disgrace to all that is human. On very simple terms, it would accept me.

He crawled forward on his belly, in a please-don't-hurt-me pose, stretching itself toward the bit of meat. Its tongue raked my fingers, a new sensation. A pleasant one.

I don't know how long we sat like that. With each morsel of food, the jackal pup came closer. As darkness fell and the night grew cold, I gathered my cloak around me. I would not travel this night. We eyed each other as the hours passed. Sometimes he would growl. Sometimes I would speak. We got used to each other's smells and sounds.

"You will need a fierce name to survive in this world," I said. "I think I will call you Cain."

Finally, wearying of exercising his courage and with a belly full of meat, Cain the jackal found a spot next to me, and we both fell asleep.

We began traveling together the next night.

I'd pour water into my hand from the goatskin, and he'd lap it up. He finished off the meat, even though it had gone too rancid for me to eat. Jackals, I learned, would eat anything, including the dates I carried.

It's useful to be versatile, in one's habits as well as in one's diet. More choices means more chances of survival.

I knew a little bit about animals.

There had been peacocks in the women's garden. The estate supported goats and sheep and chickens for the Master's table. There were horses and camels in the stable or tethered outside with one leg bound to make them docile. My mother had sent me to do chores with the stable hands, as caring for animals might be one of the things I'd need to know how to do someday. I could only go there after dark, or when my father was away, so my knowledge was limited, but I was comfortable around animals.

People were much harder.

My little jackal must have been born deformed, like me. There was no scar showing his leg had been bitten off. There was not even a bump. It was as if the Creator had gone to the storehouse for legs, dropped one on the way back, and hadn't bothered to return for it.

"Three legs are enough for this one," the Creator said, in the same way he said, "Ugliness is good enough for this one," when I was made. "She has a mouth, a nose, two eyes, and two ears—what does it matter if they are not all in the right place?"

Cain and Anubis. A killer and a god of death.

We belonged together.

Sometimes I would carry him, nestled in the crook of my arm. He had no weight to notice. He would take short puppy-naps, rocked to sleep by the rhythm of my steps on the good desert ground. When he wiggled to be put down, I placed his feet gently beside mine. We kept pace with each other.

When the water ran out, we hid and kept watch over a well belonging to some desert people. I did not know who. To steal water is a dangerous task. I had heard my father and his guests brag about people they'd run through with their swords simply for being driven by thirst to seek water wherever they could. No one was in sight of this well, but the desert is deceiving. Someone might have been hiding, waiting for me, the same way I was hiding, waiting for them.

Finally, under a night sky that was blessedly moonless, Cain and I went down to the well, raised up some water, and filled our bellies and my goatskin. We were as soundless as growth, and if the enemy spotted us, he let us go on our way.

Perhaps the stink of murder, of the damnation of my soul, acted as a repellent. Whatever. We had water.

My little jackal ate anything that moved, from insects to lizards, to small desert rats still hairless from their nests. I made him share what he caught with me. Food is food. Blood and flesh sustain, whether roasted with herbs and fragrant oil or swallowed whole, with the warmth of life still clinging to it.

We survived.

It was not always easy. Hunger and thirst are uncomfortable, even horrible, no matter where you are or who you are. There were dangers and hot days and cold nights.

But I had something in my favor.

I had no expectations.

I had no reason to believe or even hope that life would be kind, that I would ever be welcome or have a place.

Now I had a companion. My life was better than I ever thought it would be.

CHAPTER SIX

For months we went on this way. Cain grew strong and brave, and I grew brave and strong. We survived.

The desert sustains life in many forms. I could have lasted there until my old age finally took me.

The desert takes away all that is not essential. It is the gift of simplicity, of always being on the edge of extinction. It gives simple choices, between hunger and thirst, heat and chill, darkness and light.

I was alive, I was free, and anything else I left to Allah, and to the brain that the Creator gave me.

I grew harder all over.

The first weeks were spent in a haze of grief from missing my mother. After the shock of the killing and the newness of the desert wore off, my loss took over my mind. My sorrow was a heavy burden. Then, one night I woke up to a glorious red sunset and found that my burden was gone. The sun and the sand and the wide, wide sky had absorbed my pain and lifted it off me. In its place there was gratitude.

My little jackal and I lived our lives, complete with each other and needing no others.

But others, as they tend to do, intruded.

I was found in the heat of the day.

I was in a deep sleep, the sound sleep of someone who walked hard and didn't expect to meet anybody in the vast, vast land.

They crept up so stealthily that not even Cain woke up until they were standing right over us.

Cain's yelps were still the yelps of a puppy. I heard their voices register shock, then amusement.

Then I sat up, and the cloth that had been protecting my face from the harsh noon-day sun slipped from my face.

The ring of people bending over me drew back as if they had but one body.

I was scared. There were too many of them to fight, but I felt around for my father's sword. The chance of running faster than all of them was slim, but I looked for an opening anyway. When you are under threat, everything inside you focuses on survival.

For a long moment I stared at them, and they stared at me. I was about to dash straight at them, swinging my sword, when one of them spoke.

"Are you the one we've been hearing about?"

"You must be," said another. "We did not know this when we disturbed you. Please forgive us."

"Have mercy," said a third.

Their eyes all looked toward the ground, a sign of humility, of acknowledgment that they stood before one greater than themselves.

"What have you heard of me?" I demanded with an arrogance I did not feel.

"That you are a jackal in human form. That you have powers over the underworld, and you kill men in the desert as they sleep."

The man I'd left alive in the desert that night must have stayed alive, at least long enough to tell his tale. And as we all know, a tale grows with the telling.

"I only kill men who harm women," I said. "Do any of you have a quarrel with me on that?"

I moved my ugly face slowly around the semicircle of frightened people. Now that I was no longer scared, I could see more clearly who they were, a small band of nomads. A few were women, their faces undraped in the manner of some roaming peoples. I saw one woman's lips twitch into the sliver of a smile.

"How could we quarrel with such wisdom?" one man said. The other men smiled and nodded.

"We have never mistreated women, and we would also kill anyone who did!"

I didn't believe them, of course. How could I? All I had known of men up to that point was that they were instruments of brutality. Still, any advantage in the desert was worth exploiting.

I stretched out a hand and snapped my fingers. My jackal stopped yelping and came to rest at my side.

"What do you have to share with me?" I asked.

In an instant the ground in front of me was littered with a mismatched assortment of knives, cups, jewelry, bridles. "You seem to have had the good fortune of picking up a variety of things from a variety of places," I said.

"We come by these things honestly," a woman said. "We are not thieves. We are traders, trading our goats and weavings for some things, and then trading those things for other things."

I had not known there were people who lived this way. I knew very little, really, about how most people lived.

"Keep your honest goods," I said. "I need something to sustain my body, not weigh down my purse."

"We are out of water," an older woman said. "There is a well not far from here, but the owner forbids us to draw from it. He will not even let us give water to our goats or our children."

"When we saw you asleep, we hoped you had water to share with us."

"If you will consent to come with us, the well owner will let us draw what we need. He would not dare resist you."

I had a bit of water left in my goatskin. I passed it to the old woman, who doled it out to the little ones.

Now I needed water too. I was in the same situation as these people. I almost belonged. It felt good.

I doubted the well owner would listen to me, but it was worth the gamble.

All of life is a gamble anyway. You gamble when you lie down at night that the sand beneath your body does not contain a scorpion and that a snake will not slither into the folds of your garments for warmth. You gamble that you are heading closer to water, not farther away from it. Everything is chance.

"We will go when the moon rises," I said. "Until then I will sleep."

I covered my face against the sun and lay back down in the sand.

Around me, I heard the sounds of the others seeking shelter beneath their cloaks. They did not question my decision. I actually fell asleep.

They were awake and ready when I next opened my eyes.

On their faces was only trust. They believed I could protect them. They believed I could save them.

There was only one way to find out.

I stood up and brushed the sand from my cloak.

"Let's go," I said.

They knew the way to the well.

We walked together without comment, without threat or ridicule. The heat from their bodies warmed me in the cold desert night. I was surprised to not mind their company.

After some time one of the men said, "The well is just ahead. It is always guarded."

"We have never been able to drink from it," a woman told me. "We must pass this way to get to the pastures for our goats, and every year we lose some of our animals to thirst. Last year we lost a child."

No one had ever depended on me for anything before. This task changed from being a gamble for survival to being a gift I wanted to give these people.

"Give me your water bags," I said.

The goatskin bags were passed through the tribe to me. I slung them over my arm, checked that my father's sword was by my side, and covered my face with my cloak.

"Wait here," I told the tribe. I signaled my jackal to stay. He whined but obeyed.

There was enough moon to see the marker for the well. I was not cautious. I did not creep upon the water like a thief. I marched with strong steps, as strong as my body would allow.

I got to the water without interruption and began to draw water.

"This is a private well," a voice behind me said.

"Water is a gift from God," I replied, continuing to draw the water, and not turning around.

"That may be," the man said, "but the well belongs to me."

I began filling a goatskin. I heard the man pull on his sword.

"There's a strong scent here tonight," I said. "Do you smell it?"

"You are about to die for trespassing at my well, and you take the time to sniff the air?"

"Death is nothing to me," I said. "And the scent is not in the air. It is on my sword."

I finished filling one goatskin and started on another.

"You talk too much," the man said. "But never mind. Soon you will be silent."

I kept my head down, intent on my task. I was flooded with calm, and the desert sand saw not one drop of spilled water that night. I filled and secured another goatskin.

Behind me, I heard the man take a step toward me.

In the next instant, I had spun around and drawn my father's sword. I held it out before me like a lantern.

"Can you smell it now?" I asked in a calm, quiet voice.

The man had been expecting an easy kill, or at least to be faced with fear.

I had no fear. I had been left for dead a long, long time ago.

"The scent of blood never leaves my sword."

"You are living in a dream," the man said. "Your dream tells you that a little person like you can wield that sword like a proper man."

"My last dream left four men dead in the desert after they raped and murdered a woman."

I saw him flinch then. He had heard the story.

With a small movement of my hand, I summoned my jackal. Cain tore toward me like a sandstorm, barking and showing his teeth. I loved him then.

"A man who denies water to poor people in the desert is not worthy of being called a man." I let the cloth fall from my face. "Don't you agree?"

His eyes grew wide with terror. "You really exist?"

"I stand before you," I said. With a wave of my hand, I brought the rest of the tribe over to the well.

"I make you no threats," I said. "These people will pay you a fair price for the use of your well. And they will be grateful for your graciousness."

The man looked at the group and lowered his sword slightly. "Such graciousness will see people flocking to my well like flies to a dead donkey."

"And they will pay you a fair tribute for the privilege of drawing water."

I could see him calculating his impending wealth.

"Pay me ten goats," he told the tribe.

I made a movement with my hand, and Cain leaped toward the man, stopping inches from him.

"One goat," he said.

I nodded to the tribe. They reached for a sickly looking goat. In disgust I grabbed the healthiest goat by the scruff of its neck and passed it to the well owner.

"You are welcome to use my well," he said.

"In the future, deal with each other fairly, or you will have to deal with me," I told them. "Do you understand?"

They all nodded.

The tribe finished filling their water skins and put pans of water on the ground for the goats to drink. I gave water to my jackal, then drank deeply myself. Soon, we all were on our way.

Why they all obeyed me, why I was able to solve the conflict that they had not been able to solve on their own, I will never fully understand. The more I am around other people, the less I understand them.

CHAPTER SEVEN

I stayed with the tribe for almost a year.

One day drifted into another. They never asked me to leave, and it was easier to stay than go. With them I crossed the desert into pasture-land, then back across the desert again.

I pulled my weight. Cain and I would go hunting, bringing back a hare or other small game. They believed that I could always get them access to water, no matter what the foe. Fortunately, I wasn't tested again. I assisted them in bargaining for trade goods and saw that the transactions were fair to both sides.

With the women I gathered firewood and patted goat droppings into flat cakes. We dried these in the sun and used them for fuel when no other was available. They taught me about plants that were good to eat and plants that were medicine. I soothed crying babies and played finger games with the toddlers.

With the older children I tended the goats. I tried to teach them their letters, showing them how marks in the sand could translate into things they saw around them—sun, mother, jackal. They did not make much progress. They had never seen a book and believed my dirt-scratchings were part of my connection to the underworld. I dropped the writing classes, and we played games instead. I made chess and backgammon sets out of wood and stones, and everyone enjoyed those.

With the men I shared the hookah pipes at night, as the tribe sat around the fire after the evening meal. I recited the poetry of Rumi and the tales of Shaherazad. They were spellbound at my wisdom, believing this all came from my own brain. I saw no need to enlighten them.

Although I shared their lives and their labor, my jackal and I were not one of them. They could not know my history. They could not know that I was human like them, a child like their children. I kept the worst of my ugliness hidden from them by a cloth that bound my face. This was done as a kindness, but also to save the power of my grotesqueness for when it was needed. It also kept the sand out of my nose and mouth.

The fall, when it came, was swift and hard.

One of the women gave birth.

The baby was disfigured.

Its distortion was mild compared to mine, but it was enough to turn the tribe against me.

"Your ugliness is poisoning the rest of us!" the father of the beautiful new baby said.

(I call the baby beautiful because it was, they all are, and ever shall be.)

"You turned the child ugly in the womb! You are a devil who must be cast out!"

I couldn't blame them, really, as I ran for my life, holding tightly to the few possessions I'd been able to grab as soon as I saw which way the wind was blowing. Maybe they should have known better than to chase me through the desert, throwing rocks at my back, but they didn't. I was grateful for their hospitality all those months, and I was grateful that none had good aim.

On some days, that's as good as it gets.

Cain and I wandered on our own for a while. I lost track of how long.

One night my jackal heard the call of other jackals. He ran out after it, came back to me, then sat on his haunches, looking to me for some sign.

"You're mine," I said. "You can't leave me."

Then I waved him away. How could I force him to stay? He scampered off into the darkness. Soon not even the dust showed any trace that he had ever been with me.

The desert is like that. One day there will be no trace of any of us. The sand will sweep over our buildings and bones, the scrub will take root, and we will all be no more.

That's the desolate thinking that invaded my head after Cain left, and I became truly alone.

I managed to stay alive. The desert can be hospitable, in a raw, cruel way. I lived for a while in a cave, until the trickle of water nearby dried up.

Mystics live in the desert. Hermits live there. They live in states of religious purity, spending their days and nights in deep touch with the Creator.

I held no such conversations. I slept as much as possible, ate whatever came my way, and watched the sun move across the sky, creating shadows that danced a slow dance as the day went on.

I thought as little as possible.

When my dreams were good, they were filled with my mother. I would wake up sad.

When my dreams were bad, they were full of my father and the other men I killed. "You are just like us," they would say, all bloody and rancid. I would wake up sweating and long for sadness.

I suppose I was waiting to die. I had no mission, no company, and nothing to care about.

In many ways I was already dead.

So why did I start walking again when the water supply ran out?

I suppose I hadn't completely died yet.

CHAPTER EIGHT

The city of Herat appeared before me like a vision of heaven.

In my weakened, desolate state, I thought it *was* heaven. I thought that I had died and that God had made a mistake by rewarding me for a good life instead of punishing me for a bad one.

Glorious and golden, the city was. The sun made the city walls shimmer like gold.

I plopped down on the top of a hill and looked across the valley at this amazing sight.

Outside the city walls, a pageant unfolded. A camel train, hundreds of camels long, was being unloaded and tethered for the night. Groups of nomads and traders were setting up camps and feeding their livestock. I watched people going about their evening chores, getting their children and themselves settled down together before the darkness arrived.

I was far enough away that no one could see me. I kept my face uncovered to the world. I watched for hours, until the city walls turned from gold to crimson and then slipped into shadows. The moon rose, and the people disappeared. The valley floor became dotted with the lights of campfires, just like the stars in the sky.

I couldn't decide what to do. My experience with people did not make me long for their company again. But I was getting tired of my own company too. I needed an escape from myself.

In the end it was hunger that decided it.

I slipped off my hill before the sun came up. I was just another shadow as I walked through the families, tribes, and dying campfires.

I was used to being a shadow, but I confess that I wished I could have chosen a tribe, sat with them around their fire, and been made welcome. But that was not possible. I try not to dwell on what I cannot have, for that way madness lies.

I followed the road up into the city. The guards were asleep, and I did not disturb them.

A city is a miraculous thing. It is hard enough to get along with other people when there is a whole desert to share. When people are piled upon one another, as they are in a city, not just living but trying to grow and expand themselves—well, it's a miracle that there is not wholesale slaughter, every day, every hour. Whenever I begin to lose faith in people—which is often—I think about people living together in cities, not killing each other, and I think there might be hope for us.

As I entered the city, I could feel life all around me. Even though the city was mostly asleep, it throbbed. I could smell bread baking in the clay ovens, hear babies crying, hear people stirring around me. Roosters crowed, donkeys brayed, and beggars moaned as the dawn reached them on their dirt beds. Another day was beginning.

I kept my face covered and my head down. The streets began to fill up. I was just one more person. I hoped I could find food and not be noticed. I felt a little scared, but also quite exhilarated. New sights, new smells, new sounds. This, I felt oddly, was what I was born for. With so many different people all here together, maybe there was a place for me.

And then the screaming started.

Automatically, I checked my face, but it was well covered.

The screaming continued. People rushed down the street, toward me, then past me, yelling as they ran.

"It's loose! It's coming! The beast is coming!"

The ground shook, and then there was the beast.

I'd never seen anything like it. It was huge and gray, like a building of stone thundering down the avenue on legs as big as tea chests, and with ears as big as tents and a snake sticking out of the middle of its face.

Crowds rushed by, but I did not turn and join them. I was too enthralled by this magnificent thing, this giant, this vision of power and ugliness and beauty.

I stood alone in the street and watched it come closer. It was moving so quickly. I was afraid it would pass by me before my eyes grew tired of it, and that I would never see such a wonder again.

I held up my hand, to gesture for it to stop.

It ran right up to me. And stopped.

We were engulfed in a cloud of dust. The creature raised its snake-like thing and made the sound of a thousand trumpets.

"You are…tremendous," I said, reaching out my hands to convince myself through touch that what was before me was real and not just in my head.

It's flesh was rough, its energy palpable. I leaned against it, hugging it, breathing it in, feeling pure awe. All my anger at God disappeared in that moment. What did it matter that the Creator had created an abomination such as me? God had also created *this*.

I don't know how long I stood like that. I felt something touching me, stroking my back the way my mother used to do when I was upset and couldn't sleep. The long thing in the middle of the creature's face, a type of nose and arm together, was touching me. It brushed away the cloth covering my face and stroked my skin as though it was not deformed. We embraced each other.

I started to cry.

"You have a gift with the elephant, stranger," a voice said, intruding on our moment.

"Elephant." I whispered the word, and recovered my face.

"She's really very gentle and a big help with our building work on the new mosque, but some ignorant men decided to throw stones at her. They scared her. People can be cruel, you know."

I knew.

The man, older, with a long beard and gentle eyes, took hold of the nose-arm—called a trunk—and guided the elephant around.

"You have a real talent, young…forgive me, I cannot tell from your clothes if you are a young man or a young woman."

"Does it matter?" I asked, finding my voice.

"Indeed, it does not. Talent is talent, no matter the package it comes in. Tell me your name."

"Anubis," I said.

The man laughed, but it was a kind laugh. Even my untrained ear could tell the difference. "A jackal calms an elephant. Allah has blessed you, Anubis."

The elephant and the man walked back down the avenue. People flooded back into the street, giving me a wide berth. My ugliness was covered, but my strangeness still showed.

I kept still for a long, long while. It had all been so magical—the kindness. I wanted to keep the moment with me, and not disturb it by moving.

Eventually I was shoved aside by a train of heavily loaded donkeys, their backs sagging under sacks of mud bricks. I followed them farther into the city.

My hunger grew and gnawed at me. I had nothing to trade, nothing to sell. I wished I had followed the elephant and asked its keeper for a job. For a while I tried to find them, but Herat is a huge city, with streets that go in every direction. The maze swallowed me up.

Hunger raged within me, taking away caution and good sense. It was not helped by the cooking smells all around. Roadside fires grilled chunks of meat on skewers. Piles of fruit and vegetables shone with the colors of jewels near stacks of freshly baked bread. I heard the sizzle of fry-cakes sputtering in oil. To be hungry when there is no food is bad. To be hungry when there is food all around is torture.

I spied a cooking fire, temporarily abandoned. Its people were off a little ways, talking, not caring about their food because they knew they would eat. Beside the fire lay a stack of stone bread, the flat bread nomads bake on stones and city folks bake in ovens. Simmering on the fire was a pot of chickpeas and chicken, the spices filling the air and making me swoon.

If I had liked people, if people had liked me, if I'd had more sense, I could have asked. Allah instructs us all to be generous. Food would have been given to me. But I had no trust. All I had was hunger.

I crouched by the fire, grabbed a flat loaf of bread, and scooped up the stew. With not even the wits to run, I stayed on my haunches, the cloth torn from my face to give full freedom to my mouth.

Of course I was noticed.

"Thief! Thief!"

Even then I kept eating. In the split second that I *might* have gotten away, I stuffed the first helping of bread and stew into my mouth and grabbed a second. Only then did I rise to my ungainly feet and try to make my getaway.

Of course it was hopeless.

Arms grabbed at me, taking my father's sword, shaking loose the precious food, which fell to the ground and was fought over by dogs and beggars. Screams rent the air as my face was seen, the noise attracting others who added their own expressions of terror.

"I know that face!" I heard a man scream. "That is the face of the monster who killed my helpless friends in the desert! That face is the face of the most evil of all demons!"

I was beginning to regret leaving that man alive. Around me the calls for vengeance grew louder and wilder.

By then I was past caring. I shut my eyes against the ugliness of their anger and ignorance. I tried to summon the memory of my mother's voice to block out their hateful words.

My arms were bound behind me, and I was forced to my knees. There were cries for my execution. Spit and stones landed on my face and chest. I was too tired to protest, too hopeless to wish for anything but death. My belly had food in it, and I'd been treated with kindness by a wonderful creature called an elephant. Even if I was to be murdered, it had still been a good day.

My tormentors were enjoying the arguing over who would get to kill me more than, I suspected, they would enjoy the actual killing.

"Just shut up and get on with it," I said.

That's when the music started. The arguing stopped, the abuse stopped, and the sounds of drums and flutes and singing got closer and closer. I opened my eyes to see a dozen or more men playing music and dancing, swirling in ecstasy, and singing prayers to God. I had never seen such a group before, but I knew from my mother's tales that they were dervishes, Sufi masters who work themselves into an ecstasy of praise, song, and dancing. I saw my captors staring at this spectacle, mouths open, stones falling through their opening fists to the ground.

With my assassins' attention focused elsewhere, and with absolutely nothing to lose, I did the only sensible thing there was to do.

I ran.

CHAPTER NINE

You can imagine the sight.

A filthy young woman, as ugly as the devil and twice as crazy, tearing up the city street with her hands bound behind her back.

My plan to blend in was not working.

There were no thoughts in my head now, no plans, no ideas, certainly no hope. I ran simply because I still could.

I had a good head start. It took my executioners a few moments to react, but their yelling, coupled with me being the obvious escapee, soon had a lot of people chasing me. I didn't waste time looking back, but I could hear their yells and the stamp of their feet on the streets. My gait is ungainly when I have two arms to help me balance. With both pulled behind me, I must have looked comical indeed.

No matter. I kept running, knocking over vegetable stands, smashing into pyramids of copper pots, sending caged chickens and pigeons into paroxysms of fury.

I didn't really believe I would escape them, but it was almost fun trying.

"If you want to kill me, you're going to have to work for it," I sputtered between pants.

Luckily my mind is more agile than my body. Messages from my eyes go quickly to my brain. I ducked and spun. Around a corner I spied some sacks stacked up against a high wall. I took two leaps and threw myself over to the other side, into the bushes.

I landed on my back. For the first few moments all I could do was struggle to catch my breath. Down in the dirt, making myself small and low like a worm, I heard the yelling mob head my way. Their feet thundered on the ground, beasts in stampede, as they sped past my hiding place. I heard their shouts of hatred, their eagerness for my blood, coming closer and then fading away. I wanted them to keep on running, running, until they all just died.

"Monsters," I said. "The world is full of monsters."

I kept still, catching my breath. I was in no hurry to move. Even though my position was uncomfortable, I'd landed among cool, green plants, and the ground beneath me was soft. I peered out at the next world I'd have to battle with, and saw more green, with patches of color. Clearly I'd landed in a garden.

Between the stalks I could see bits of people, moving slowly, talking softly. Sometimes the sound of laughter reached my ears, mixed with birdsong. The laughter was pleasant, not mean, and the sound of the birds was kind. We take our comfort where we can. Not being immediately under attack, I fell asleep.

"Oh, look at you."

A kind, calm voice reached me through my sleep.

"You are so very beautiful."

Whoever was talking was not talking to me.

"You will look so lovely, decorating our dining table."

I almost laughed at the image of myself as a decoration. I opened my eyes to see a man moving closer and closer to me. His face was mild and dreamy, with a close, dark beard. He wore simple but adequate robes. I remember thinking how clean he looked.

He came close to my thicket, and I tried to make myself smaller among the plants. I stayed very still.

He looked not at me but at something above me. He stood at the edge of my garden bed, leaned in, and pressed his face into a branch laden with almond blossoms.

"Some say you are late this year, but how can a flower be late? The timing of a flower is always right."

He reached into the folds of his robe and brought out a small knife. "I hope you will forgive me for taking some of you away." He leaned right over me, talking to the flowers, taking a few cuttings from the tree. When he had all the blossoms he wanted, he let the knife fall from his fingers, as if, since he had no further need of it, it ceased to exist. Then he looked right down at me, with nothing in his face but kindness and happiness, and said, "Beautiful, aren't they?"

I wiggled and strained, and managed to take hold of the knife.

"Talking to the plants again, Bihzad?"

I heard a big, jovial voice, and then I saw a big, jovial face, gaping down at me in astonishment. He was a giant of a man, a mountain on legs, large in stature and in the swirl of energy around him.

"We are so fortunate to be surrounded by such beauty," the mild one called Bihzad said, holding the blossoms in front of the face of his companion.

The big, hairy head shook in amazement. "My friend, I worry about you sometimes." To me, he asked, "What manner of creature are you?"

The question was asked without malice and came from a face without hate. I twisted some more, to make visible my bound arms, and offered him the knife.

"'Do not look at my outward shape, but take what is in my hand,'" I quoted.

"A monster who recites the words of the great poet Rumi," the hairy one said. "What is your name, monster?"

"My name is for those who do not call me monster."

That is the first time I heard the great, soul-lifting laugh of Haji Dost Muhammad. "Would I be right in assuming that your arms are so arranged against your will?"

"Well, I did not tie myself up in this fashion," I replied.

"Then perhaps you will permit me to cut through the ties that bind."

In a moment my hands were free. I scrambled to my feet. These strangers seemed kind, but I needed to be able to flee if they should turn out to be normal men.

Haji introduced himself. "I am Haji Dost Muhammad, painter, inventor, and adventurer." He gave a little bow, possibly making fun, but I sensed a good spirit. "And this," he said, his great arm around the thin shoulder of his dreamy friend, "this is Kamal al-Din Bihzad."

He announced it in grand fashion, as though he were proclaiming a sultan. Bihzad also bowed amicably.

"May we now have the pleasure of your name?" Bihzad asked.

"I am Anubis," I said.

"The Egyptian jackal, the god of the dead. You have come out of the underworld?"

"I have come out of the desert."

"You looked like you have brought the desert with you."

I turned to go. I knew I was dirty. I was not interested in having these men lord their cleanliness over me.

Then I heard the thunder again, the mobile wave of hatred, yelling for my blood. It pounded on the gate of the garden, near where we were standing.

I didn't pause to give explanation or ask permission. I dived into the deepest clump of bushes just as a servant opened a door in the gate and the sound of murder invaded the green stillness, loud and clear.

Haji's voice was louder than the mob's. "Good evening," he said. "Peace be upon you."

"And upon you. We are looking for the monster, the bloodthirsty creature who strikes down innocent men in the desert and feasts upon their flesh. We had it captured, but it got away."

I tried to make myself smaller.

"That sounds like quite a monster," I heard Haji say.

"What is this noise?" I heard the voice of another man, approaching us from a garden path. I saw a vibrant red cloak and a pointed beard as he moved past my bushes to the open gate.

"These men are saying a monster is on the loose," Haji said.

"It killed ten men in the desert, good shepherds, mild and kind, and now it is here in Herat. None of us is safe until the monster is recaptured and its head removed from its body."

"My dear Qalam, it seems we are in danger," Haji said to the man in the red robe.

"Nonsense!" said this man, Qalam. "The monsters come from your own abuse of wine, your own indulgence in opium. We are artists here, and if you disturb us again, I will have you all thrown in jail, in the name of the Sultan!"

I couldn't believe it when the gate clanged shut and the mob went on its way.

"You are a fool to waste your time with fools," Qalam said.

"Then I will bid you good evening," Haji said. I saw the red disappear into the green of the garden. Haji returned to Bihzad, who was standing not far from me.

Calm returned to the garden. I crawled out of the bushes. Bizhad looked troubled. Haji looked amused.

"I take it they were looking for you," Haji said. "Did you really do those things?"

The accusations were so outlandish that I was able to say truthfully, "No. But I would be grateful for a few hours' sanctuary and a cloak to cover myself."

"I think we can do better than that, can't we, Bihzad? We have baths here, the best of food and drink, and clothes that will keep you warm."

"Do you think Mir Ali Shir would mind?" Bihzad asked Haji. "The Vizier is our sponsor. He created this colony for artists and thinkers. I would not want to go against his intention. Should we not merely give alms, as is our duty?"

"You are the greatest living painter of miniatures," Haji said. "I am sure the Vizier would agree to any request that came from you. Still, perhaps Anubis is an artist. Do you have any special talent?" he asked me.

"I have a talent for staying alive," I replied. "Feed me or don't. My life is my own." I turned away again.

"Oh, what a perfect creature, just the thing to relieve my current boredom! So amusing! Bihzad, you have in your hand a sprig of flowers because their beauty inspires you to create even greater beauty. Anubis is just like a sprig of flowers, sent to stimulate our minds and talents."

Now it was my turn to be amused. What manner of creatures were *these*? It might be worth putting up with some foolishness to find out. Besides, I could use a meal and a bath, and something to cover myself.

Bihzad was satisfied with Haji's explanation. "Then let us get our new friend settled and introduced to the colony."

"No, no, secrecy is best. Not all of our colleagues are as welcoming as we are."

"I'm sure you are wrong," Bihzad said.

"You're so good, you never notice those who aren't. I am not such a saint. We need a plan."

Night proper had arrived, and with it the desert cold.

"Could your plan possibly come with a cloak?" I asked, shivering in the thin shift the mob left me wearing.

"We are fools," Bihzad said. "Forgive us."

I followed the two men down the garden path. We had gone but a few steps when Haji stopped and turned to me. "If you did not commit those crimes, why were your arms bound behind your back? Why were they chasing you?"

"They were jealous of my good looks," I replied.

The two men stared at me for a stunned moment, then Haji laughed his big, booming laugh. Even Bihzad smiled. Life and death are a joke to those with safe body and full purse.

I didn't care. I'd escaped my executioners. The ground was soft beneath my bare and battered feet, and the flowers around me smelled sweet. Pleasures, when they come, are to be savored.

The garden we walked through was a remarkable achievement of harmony and beauty. I was in too much of a state of shock then to be able to notice the details, but even so its soothing properties reached me. The night-blooming flowers were releasing their perfume. I breathed deeply. Their scent was better than food. I heard quiet voices from different pockets of the garden, muffled by plants, and servants came out and lit oil lamps.

Haji and Bihzad steered me into a small garden within the garden, a room within a room, one stone bench surrounded by growth, hidden and private. "Please wait here a moment. We will return with a woman who will assist us."

They left me. I waited in the shadows.

A servant put down a tray on a stool near the alcove where I stood. On it were small pieces of bread, spread with something fragrant. As soon as he left them unattended, I stepped out of the shadow, bent over the tray, and picked up as many of the pieces as I could. I had the dish nearly empty when I heard his footsteps and ducked back out of sight.

If my mouth hadn't been so full, I would have laughed at the expression on his face when he saw the nearly empty tray. He shook his head, picked up the tray, and headed back into the building.

"Where are you going? Did you eat that food?" I heard an angry male voice say.

"No, Master. The food just disappeared. I am going back to the kitchen now to refill the tray."

"Food doesn't just disappear. You ate it, and now you're lying about it." The two men stepped into the light. The one doing all the yelling was the man in the red robe who had answered the mob at the gate. The servant hung his head. "Show me where you left it."

"Right here, on this stool, Master."

"And you expect me to believe that some creature came and ate the food. You're a fool to think I'd believe that."

"Master, I…"

The man in the red robe slapped the servant across the face. "How dare you speak to me! Get back to work! If you steal more food, I'll have you whipped!"

The servant hurried away. I watched the man in the red robe join a group across the garden, acting just as pleasant as could be. I chewed and swallowed the food in my mouth and hoped I'd have the opportunity to make it up to the servant.

Haji and Bihzad returned, accompanied by a woman. Her head was covered but her face was unveiled, and her dress, like Bihzad's, was simple but adequate.

"My name is Maryam," she said to me quietly, extending her hand for me to grasp. Her face registered neither shock nor revulsion.

"I am Anubis, and I am filthy."

"I spend my days in clay," she replied. "Dirt does not scare me."

"Maryam works in ceramics," Bihzad said. "Her work is exquisite."

"My work falls short," Maryam said, "but that concern is put away until tomorrow. Come. Let's get you settled."

"Wait—where will she stay?" Haji asked. "Will she be welcomed among the other women?"

Maryam wasn't sure, but "if it is Bizhad's wish that she stay with us, they will not object."

"Not objecting is not the same as welcoming," Haji said. "Go, bathe and get comfortable. My friend and I will come up with something."

With nothing to lose, I followed Maryam into the next stage of my life.

CHAPTER TEN

Maryam put her arm around my humped shoulders, a gesture of such kindness it was almost painful. We passed under several archways, through several hallways, and across courtyards and bridges, finally coming to a separate, low building.

"Here are the women's quarters," Maryam said. "It is small because there are only a few of us. Wait here a moment. I will make sure we have privacy."

I slid into a shadow. Maryam returned quickly and took me inside.

"What sort of a place is this?" I asked her.

"A good place to work. We can concentrate on our skills and ideas without the distractions most women have to contend with. And most of the other artists are enlightened and treat us as equals."

"Except for the man with the pointed beard," I said. "I saw him mistreat a servant."

Maryam nodded. She knew who I meant. "That is Muhammad Siyah Qalam. He is called the Black Pen because he does drawings and calligraphy in black ink. I suppose he's talented or he wouldn't be here, but his talent doesn't extend to his humanity."

"Perhaps it would assist him to gain wisdom if he had to serve himself for a time," I suggested. A quick smile flashed across Maryam's face as she led me into the cleaning room. Before long I was languishing in a bath. Out of pity for her and her servants, I told them I preferred to bathe in private. It's bad enough that I have to see myself without clothes.

I had been in the desert a long time, but I still remembered how to use lotions and soaps, and I emerged from the water much cleaner and sweeter smelling.

New clothes had been laid out for me. They were simple garments, like Bihzad's and Maryam's. There was an outer cloak, woven with camel hair for warmth; a linen over-dress; and a plain cotton shift. A linen head covering was laid out for me too. I draped it over my head and affixed it so it covered the worst of my face.

I headed out of the private area, looking for where the others had gathered. Even if they turned me out onto the street, I was ahead of where I had been earlier. It was exhilarating to be so free of worries and hopes. Sometimes life moves very fast, and all we can do is ride along with it.

The complex was like Herat, full of twists and turns. I found and followed the scent of food, then lost it again.

I moved deep into one of the larger buildings. Narrow hallways opened up onto larger rooms, and broke off again into passageways. Even in the lantern light I could tell the rooms were all beautiful, rich with tile work and fabric, quiet with color and carved stone.

Then I came to a room that was different from the others. A single torch burned, but it shed enough light to let me see the vibrancy of the many colors in the paintings that lined the walls and shelves. The paintings were small, and they drew me in for a closer look.

There were animal scenes, battle scenes, and portraits of people enjoying conversation in the gardens. I bent low over them for a better look.

"Poor efforts, I know, but we do what we can."

At the sound of a man's voice, I spun around to see Bihzad in the doorway. I relaxed a little.

"I don't think they're poor efforts at all," I said. "I think they're wonderful."

"There is so much more to learn, so much yet we are unable to do, with color, with design, with balance...." His voice trailed away as he picked up a painting and stared at it.

"I smelled food," I said after a fairly long silence.

"Oh, yes, you must be hungry. Haji has come up with a good idea. We have a small house at the far end of the garden, a place for storage. He's there now, getting it ready."

We went back out into the garden. The shadows and plants provided cover, and no one disturbed us.

The garden was vast, with canals and bridges, ponds and galleries. The perimeter walls were lined with cypress trees and sweet-smelling vines.

"It's so restful," I said.

"Are you in need of rest?" Bihzad asked.

"I have been wandering for a long time."

"Then I hope you will stay for a long time, and when you are rested, you can tell me all you've learned from your wandering."

He was so kind, and the garden was so beautiful, and my life was so full of crime. I had a sudden urge to blurt out the whole awful truth of my life.

Luckily we came to the end of our garden journey before I could do anything foolish.

"Ah, there you are!" Haji stood in front of a small house, a hut, really, stuck at the back garden wall. "Will this do?"

Servants had piled pots and tools off to a side of the small yard where the shed sat, I accepted Haji's invitation to enter.

The shed had been only roughly cleaned, but it was small and cozy, with a mat for sleeping and a stool for sitting on in the sun. "It's a little like a hermit's cave," I said with pleasure. It would absolutely do.

"A hermit! Perfect. You will be a wandering hermit, a pilgrim, guest of the great Bihzad," Haji said. "No one can argue with that."

I thanked the servants who were still around, completing the transformation.

"I hope you will be comfortable here," Bihzad said. Then his face broke into a smile. He was looking above and beyond me.

"I see you!" he said, going past me and standing by the hut. A kitten sat on the rooftop, just above Bihzad's head. He reached up and brought the mewing animal into his arms. "I've been looking for you!"

He held the kitten out to me. "Could you hold her still? This will just take a moment."

I had no idea what he was talking about, but I was happy to cradle the kitten. The mewing stopped and became loud purring. I held her up to my ear, to hear it better, and she licked an uncovered spot on my face.

I so much prefer animals to people.

Bihzad reached over and quickly plucked some hairs from the

kitten's back. The kitten started, but I rubbed her ears and she became contented again.

"I'd better take advantage of her stillness," Bihzad said, plucking out more hairs and securing them all in a bit of cloth. "I spend more time chasing her than I do painting."

I was still puzzled but didn't enquire further, as a servant was approaching with a tray of food.

"It's late, so we'll leave you to your meal," Haji said. They all bade me good night, and I was left alone in my new house.

I took the stool into the yard and balanced the tray on my knees. The night was fine, the food was good. I ate with joy, then went inside and quickly fell asleep.

I slept well that night and woke at my leisure, with the fine sun making patterns on the walls of my little hut. The blanket was almost too warm on me now that the day was here, but I felt so cozy and comfortable, I was reluctant to remove it.

I supposed I should be on my way. They had offered me sanctuary for the night, and it would be ungracious of me to take advantage of that.

Still, a thought danced at the back of my mind that maybe, just maybe, after all the blood and wandering, I had finally come to a place of safety. I decided to try to stay for a few days. The desert would always be there.

I stretched my tired but clean body and got off the mat. I felt fine in my new clothes, and I hoped I would be able to keep them.

"Be careful, fool! You'll spill it!"

I heard footsteps and an angry voice heading my way, so I quickly wound the cloth over my head and stood in the doorway to greet whatever was coming, ready to run if that was necessary.

The man with the pointed beard, the one Maryam called Qalam, or the Black Pen, was headed toward me.

"Peace be with you," he said.

I bowed my covered head in response.

He gave sharp, curt orders to the servants, who set up a little table with food and drink, then dismissed them with a snarl. I wanted to yell out my thanks to them but decided to hold my tongue.

"The news of your arrival has spread through our little colony," he said. "We are gratified to have the presence of a pilgrim. I know you being here will raise the level of thought and behavior."

I bowed again, wanting him to go away so I could eat, but he kept talking.

"We are the elite of Persia, and our great gifts also give us great responsibility. Unfortunately, some members of the community think this just gives them greater license to offend the natural order and take advantage of their benefactors."

On and on he talked, strutting like a cockerel and keeping me from my breakfast. The covering over my face allowed me to make my grotesque features even more grotesque, in his honor. I thought about tossing back my face cover and rushing out at him with a scream, but I wanted to remain in this green world awhile longer.

In the middle of Qalam's pious talk, Maryam came into the clearing. She bowed respectfully to Qalam and said, "I heard that the Vizier's assistant is looking for you."

"The Vizier?" The Black Pen straightened his back and his turban, and spun around, barely remembering to bid me good-bye before hurrying out of the clearing.

"He likes being thought important by important people," Maryam said, smiling. "I hope you don't mind me sending him away. I find him tiring."

"I'm glad he left," I said.

"I see you have been served with breakfast already," Maryam said, looking at my tray. "Is there anything else you need?"

"Do you have a strip of cloth I can wrap around my face? This hood provides some coverage, but it's not complete."

"We have lots of cloth here," she said. "That's an easy request to fulfill. Now, please, enjoy your breakfast. I leave you to the peace of the garden."

I wouldn't have minded more of her company, but I am easily contented. The birds were singing, the flowers were blooming, and I ate every morsel on the tray.

CHAPTER ELEVEN

After breakfast my fatigue overtook me again, and I went back inside the hut to sleep. I did not know how long this sanctuary would last, and my body responded to my sudden feeling of safety by taking as much rest as it could. I slept a lot those first few days at the colony.

When I woke again, it was afternoon. A lunch of bread and olives was on my bench, and also a gift of winding cloths from Maryam. I hoped no one had seen my face while I slept, but I assumed not, since I was not awakened by screams.

I ate my lunch, bound my face, then ventured out into the garden, curious to see in what manner of place I had landed.

The gardens, places of endless calm and delight, wove in and among a collection of buildings that flowed smoothly into one another. Each building was beautifully decorated with intricate designs around the doors in tile and paint. Through glories of light and design, small vistas seemed big and large spaces seemed intimate. All was harmony, and color, and flowing, happy water.

In the heat of the day, most of the colony was at rest, so I was able to enjoy my walk undisturbed. Small gatherings of men lay in the shade or under canopies, smoking hookahs or sleeping. They took no notice of me.

I spotted Bihzad. He was sitting on the side of a stone pond, sprinkling crumbs of food into the water for the fish.

"Do you ever wonder what fish think about?" he asked, as I sat beside him on the edge of the pond.

I looked down into the water, where the large orange and white fish darted among the plants. Bihzad seemed in no hurry for an answer. He sprinkled more food, and the fish rose to eat.

"I have lived my life apart from fish," I replied. "I'd like to know the answer to your question, but first I'd have to spend more time with them. If all fish know is water, could they possibly think about anything else?"

"All we humans know is life on the ground, here and now, yet our minds take us to infinite times and places."

"Would our minds continue to do so if we lived underwater?"

We trailed our fingers in the pond. The fish came to nibble at our fingertips, then swam away again, disappointed that we weren't food.

I looked up to see Bihzad looking at me. I could see the kindness in his face, mixed with the vagueness I had seen before. He gave the impression of looking at one thing but seeing something completely different.

"Are you rested?" he asked.

"I am," I told him. "And I'd like to thank you for allowing me to…"

I didn't finish my sentence. He waved away my gratitude. It wasn't necessary.

"You are welcome to all we have. Haji thinks we should be secretive about your presence, but I disagree. Giving sanctuary is our duty. Is there some work you would like to do while you are within these walls? No life can be complete without useful labor."

So I was to be a servant here, then. In such a place as this, the work could not be too unpleasant, as long as I did not have to serve the Black Pen.

"I have some experience with animals," I began, not really expecting that Bihzad had any jackals that needed training or charging elephants that needed calming.

"Then you must begin at the library," he said excitedly. "You have not seen it yet, have you? I have lived with it all my life, yet it never fails to fill me with awe."

He was off down the garden path before I had even risen to my feet. I hurried after him, still puzzled but finding his excitement contagious.

"Of course it grows all the time. The Sultan and his men go on trips, and they come back with new volumes. The cataloguers are always busy, but what a happy way to be busy!"

We left the garden, turning into one of the buildings. We went down a corridor, made a turn, went through a high set of doors—and there we were.

For a long while I could not breathe. Never had I imagined that such a place could exist. The few books in my father's house had not prepared me for the glory that was now before me.

Shelves and shelves of books and scrolls. Books bound in leather and books bound in wood. Books strewn on tables and stacked on floors. Everywhere, books.

There were people too, men and women, sitting on stools, standing at the shelves, propped up against cushions on carpets over the floor. They read, they paused in thought, and they whispered ideas to themselves as they sat with the books, too absorbed in their study to notice the midday heat.

"We have more than a thousand volumes of the Quran," Bihzad whispered to me. "We have over sixty thousand books on science, poetry, philosophy, and literature. We have books with great ideas and small, good ideas and bad. And more come in all the time."

The numbers swarmed in my head. All my hungers and all my thirsts paled in comparison to this new appetite, for knowledge.

"Let me introduce you to the librarian." He drew me near an old man bent low over a thick volume. "This is Anubis," he said, "a pilgrim who will be our guest for a while and who will be using the library from time to time."

The old man nodded, as polite as was necessary but clearly not wanting to take his eyes off the book. I understood that then, and I understand it now. Our time with books is limited, but books are not.

"Come and see the rest of the complex." Bihzad led the way again. I marked in my own mind the turnings to the library, so that I would be able to find it again.

We passed by a room where the Black Pen was kicking at a servant. I stopped at the entrance, thinking we should stop him, but Bihzad moved on, not even noticing. The servant ran past me out of the room, the Black Pen tossing something at his head. He recognized me from my clothes, put on a revolting smile, and bowed low. I bowed back, then caught up with Bihzad.

We went from room to room, building to building. Everywhere there were people—mostly men but also women—reading, or painting, or writing, or making pottery, or transcribing books with calligraphy so beautiful that each letter was like its own painting.

Bihzad introduced me to some of the people we met. "This is Yari, a calligrapher," or "This is Kwandamir, an historian." Others were painters, designers, or artisans working with tile. In return they would bow and say, "Peace be unto you, Master."

"Did you earn all of this with your painting?" I asked Bihzad.

"Earn? I don't know what you mean."

"You own this place, do you not?"

He laughed, a pleasant sound. "A very entertaining mistake you have made," he said. "I own nothing. I am just a servant, a slave, a prisoner."

"But the others call you Master."

Bihzad waved the word away with the back of his hand. "They do so out of kindness," he said. "It means nothing."

I knew there was more to it. I had seen slaves, and servants, and prisoners, and he was none of those things.

"Do you drink coffee?" Bihzad asked me.

"Yes," I said. I hadn't before, but this seemed like a good time to try new things. He spoke to a servant, then led us to a carpet on the ground with cushions to lean against.

"The Sultan Husayn, a most generous man, built this atelier, or colony, and invited artists and scholars to come and work in it. There are more than two hundred of us here now."

"And you live here all the time?"

"Our work keeps us busy."

"When did you come?" I asked, trying but failing to imagine him having a normal life.

"I came here as a child," he said. "My parents died when I was very small. I was raised by Amir Ruhallah Mirak Hiravi, the great calligrapher, and grew up in this complex. It was smaller then. It has grown. It grows all the time."

"And now you paint miniatures."

"In my very poor way," he replied.

They all talked like that, I was to learn, always speaking words of humility when it came to discussions of their talents. Some of them meant the words. Others didn't. Bihzad meant them.

Haji joined us on the carpet.

"I've told Qalam that you have taken a vow of silence," Haji whispered to me. "It's a nice dramatic touch, don't you agree? You will forgive us, then, for not requesting that you respond to us in public spaces. We will save our conversations for more private times, all right?"

That was fine with me, and I wasn't in a position to bargain anyway. Others joined us on the carpet, those not privy to our secret. I, usually so full of opinions and so eager to share them, was for once content to sit, listen, and learn. I wondered which among them would joyfully turn me in to the mob once they saw my monstrous features. We all wear masks, and often masks of compassion and intellect hide true meanness and cowardice. For all their fine thoughts and words and talents, most, I'd no doubt, would equate ugliness with evil and not be able to make the leap beyond it.

The servants came with coffee in an urn, a collection of small cups, and a plate of cakes. Bihzad thanked them and did the pouring himself.

I took a cup of the hot, brown-black liquid and accepted a lump of sugar from the bowl he offered. The scent of the coffee was pleasant. I watched Bihzad to see what he would do.

He took a taste of the sugar, then sipped the coffee. I did the same. The coffee was bitter, but the sugar took most of the bite from it. The drink invigorated me. I smiled and settled back on the cushion to drink the rest.

The Black Pen joined us. I thought I read in his brooding face that he was surprised to see a pilgrim, supposedly pious, taking social time with those he considered less pure. If he had those thoughts, he kept them to himself. But I saw his eyes narrow when I took a second cake, and I was glad I wasn't dependent on him for my survival.

******

"Does your ugliness disturb you?"

The question, asked in a voice that was curious, not cruel, came from Maryam. Older than I was, but younger than my mother, Maryam had a kind, serious face. We were sharing a meal.

I stopped eating the yogurt and almonds to think for a moment. "The reaction of other people disturbs me," I said. "When I lived in the desert, I never thought about it. My companion was a jackal, and he liked me anyway. I only have to think of the way I look when I am with other people."

Maryam refilled my teacup and poured some for herself. The minty steam rose up between us.

"I have always been glad not to be considered beautiful," she said. I almost choked, as her face was very attractive, compared to mine and to most. "It was a struggle to be allowed to come here. If there had been any hope of marriage for me, I would have had a very different life."

"Being thought substandard has its advantages," I agreed. I did not tell her that, as a nonperson, I would not have been married anyway. Other things, equally bad and even worse, would have happened to me if I had not been so repulsive.

One night soon after, my body caught up on its rest. I couldn't sleep anymore. I wandered out into the delight of the garden at night.

My wanderings took me into the labyrinth of buildings, and I went from room to room, marveling at what had been created.

"No, no, kitten. These are not for you to play with." I heard Bihzad's gentle voice and went in that direction.

I emerged from the labyrinth into the room full of paintings again. Bihzad was sitting on the ground, surrounded by lanterns, gently nudging the inquisitive kitten out of the way of the paint pots. I lifted the kitten into my arms and out of his way.

He leaned over a painting board that was propped at an angle. I saw he was adding paint with one of the hairs he had taken from the kitten.

"That's how you get the details so small and perfect," I whispered.

"Small, yes, but never perfect. Perfection I leave to Almighty Allah. I only hope I do not displease him too much."

I could not see how God could be displeased with someone using his talents to create something so beautiful. Then I remembered the elephant, and that my quarrels with God were at an end.

I sat beside Bihzad and watched him paint. He did not ignore me or dismiss me, or mind me being there.

For a while I thought I wanted to cry, but decided I didn't. All I wanted to do was be.

"We must prepare ourselves for the time to come in which there will be none of the things we are used to," I whispered.

"Rumi knew what he was talking about," Bihzad whispered back.

The kitten fell asleep in my arms. I let the kindness and the peace of the moment infuse me, and I did not worry about tomorrow.

CHAPTER TWELVE

It is remarkable, when I think about it, how adaptable we are. I have lived many lives, just to this point in my story, and went on to live many more, and likely still have more ahead of me; yet I have been able to find a place for myself in each new world.

I had no expectations. I felt as if I had fallen into a mythical world, one of calmness and kindness. Either I was dreaming or everyone else was. Either I would wake up or all of them would, and it would all come crashing to an end. Until then, I decided to just accept it and enjoy it. After all, I had no other plans.

The place I found for myself in Bihzad's world was among the books, at least initially. It was a good place to start. I spent my days reading and thinking, and keeping out of everyone's way. I wasn't afraid of crossing anyone—I could certainly hold my own against people armed with only wits and tongues—but I wanted to buy some time for myself. I knew I would likely be asked to leave at some point. Whatever was ahead for me, it could only be made easier by learning all that I could. My mother had taught me that.

At first I read randomly, sampling words from one book and then another. Then I decided to focus, as Bihzad had suggested, on the studies that had been done so far on animals and the science of their lives.

I found a bestiary, written two hundred years ago by Bakhtisir in Baghdad, translated from Arabic into Persian, although I could read both languages. It was full of pictures and information about animals. Some animals I had heard of, like lions and camels. Some were completely new to me, like the giant birds of the islands on the equator, big enough to carry an elephant in their claws. I remembered the elephant I had seen, and how big it was, and tried to imagine the size a bird would have to be in order to be able to carry it.

I read things about jackals that were, from my experience, completely wrong. I asked the librarian for writing materials, and I wrote down what I knew to be true. I dated my notes, and put them among the pages of inaccuracies, so readers would know that my truths were the most recent.

While my main reading was on animals, I also branched off from time to time into philosophy, science, and poetry. The library was a great one, likely one of the greatest in the world, and I wanted to read as much of it as possible in whatever amount of time I'd be allowed to continue there.

I had no way of knowing whether most of what I read was true or not. Some of it made sense. A lot of it left me with questions. I kept reading. I must confess, I looked forward to reading something I knew about more than the writer. But that happened only the one time. One time was enough, though, to teach me to read everything with suspicion. I'd found one mistake. There had to be others, even if I couldn't yet recognize them as such.

You might think my tale has become rather boring at this point. After all, going from grisly murders in the desert and encounters with raging elephants to poring over books looking for mistakes must seem like a comedown in excitement levels. Too bad. This is *my* story, and I was tired of blood-pounding excitement.

And, in its own quiet way, life at the artists' compound provided its own type of drama.

"It is a place concerned with ideas," Bihzad said during one of our talks at the hut.

"Everyone here is dedicated to finding excellence in what he or she does, be it study, or painting, or poetry. There are no other concerns. Our daily pain comes from knowing we will never attain that excellence."

I didn't think much of Bihzad's definition of pain, but I let it pass. Anyone who has lost their family carries a large pain, deep inside. I liked Bihzad. He may never have known hunger, but he had known loneliness, no matter how kind the people had been who brought him up.

"There are no rivalries?" I asked. I knew the answer, but I wanted to see what he would say. His reply was in keeping with what I knew of his character.

"How can there be rivalry when we are all dedicated to the same thing? We are brothers and sisters of the spirit, with our art and our quest to bind us."

Good, kind Bihzad. He wouldn't notice the knives of his companions even if they were buried in his back.

The others treated him with respect and deference, as I have mentioned, even though he was much younger than most of the other artists and scholars. I wondered at this, until one afternoon when I wandered into his painting studio.

My mind was full of things I had read that day, theories of gravity and theories of government. There was too much in my head to want to be alone with my thoughts, yet it was all still too confusing to discuss with anyone. Bizhad's company, cloaked in acceptance whether we talked or whether we were silent, was exactly what I needed.

I found him in his studio. Many other painters were there, leaning over their work. Bihzad was going from artist to artist, talking to them all.

"Our paintings are small, but they do not have to be crowded," he told everyone. "What would be excessive in a large canvas would be even more excessive in a small one. There is enough chaos in the world. No need to have it showing up in our paintings."

I wasn't sure how Bihzad knew anything of the world's chaos, having grown up in this enclosed, orderly environment, but I kept quiet and listened to him talk.

"With each stroke of the brush, we must say many things. We are telling not only the story, but the story behind the story. The animals, the sky, the very rocks and trees we paint must reflect that."

"A rock is just a rock," I heard one painter grumble. "The average reader won't know the difference."

Bihzad heard. "And who is the average reader of whom you speak with such derision? Is it not a man or a woman who has been blessed with the capacity to learn to read and has dedicated himself or herself to doing so? Does not the very best of their effort deserve the very best of our effort? And what of the person who cannot read, whose talents or circumstance has not permitted it? Is he or she not worthy of the great stories in the books we illustrate?"

I had never seen him like this. Nor, judging from their expressions, had many of the others. He paced back and forth across the room, all mildness gone, all humility set aside.

"Who here would like to say to an illiterate person, 'It doesn't matter if you don't understand what we are painting. You are less important than those who can read the words'? Is there anyone here who would do this?"

He glared from face to face. No one moved.

He softened, then, a little. "My dear friends, why are we here? Not just in this studio, or this colony, or even in this magnificent city that surrounds us? I mean, why are we here, in this world?"

There were several possible answers to this, the question of all questions. What is the meaning of life? Most answers are flippant, or can be spoken correctly though without conviction. "We are here to serve God," or "We are here to serve others."

But Bihzad did not have a shred of flippancy in his body. He spoke softly now.

"We are here, my friends, because there is no place else for us in the universe. The Almighty in his wisdom has found a home for us in this world, and here we be, with no more protection than a baby, and no more comfort than the sun and the moon. We are all alone, except for our God, and for the gifts that are our blessing. That's all we have."

He raised his voice again and looked hard at the man who had grumbled. "And to say we can settle for making a rock be just a rock, when we can at least try to make it mean much more, is to turn our back on those gifts. Then we are all alone but for God. And what if God turns his back on us? We would become truly alone."

He started to cry then, and strode from the studio, brushing past me in the doorway. I watched the faces of those who remained and saw reflected back expressions of awe, shame, disgust, and embarrassment. Some were embarrassed, I think, that one of their own could be overtaken by such emotion.

I hurried after Bihzad. I found him sitting on the wall of the fishpond, sobbing. I took a seat on the wall beside him. We sat together for a long while before he calmed himself and spoke.

"From time to time, a powerful loneliness overtakes me."

"The worst part about such loneliness," I said softly, "is the fear that nothing and no one will ever fill that hole in our soul."

He turned toward me a little and wiped his eyes. "Who are you lonely for?" he asked.

"My mother," I said, seeing her face in my mind as I spoke about her. "She was the bravest woman who ever lived, and she taught me that my ugliness is not an excuse, not for me and not for anyone."

"Does she still live?"

"My father killed her," I said. It was on the tip of my tongue to tell him of my own crime, but I held it back.

Bihzad fluttered his tear-wet fingers in the pond. I watched the fish rise to investigate.

"What do we do with our pain?" he asked me. "How do we survive?"

Most of my life, especially since I started wandering, had been about survival, about meeting the challenge of one more day in order to stay alive and meet the challenge again the next day. But Bihzad didn't have to worry about physical survival. He was talking about a survival much more complex than I could understand then. I can barely understand it now. But then, as now, there is still only one answer to his question.

"The best we can," I said.

CHAPTER THIRTEEN

I liked my life in the little hut, for however long it was going to last.

I soon knew all the servants by name, and often their history as well. I remembered the languages I had learned in the women's enclosure and was able to practice them with several members of the household who were captured in war and brought to Herat to serve the great minds of Persia.

Maryam came to visit when she could tear herself away from her work. Her focus was tinged with desperation, as though she might at any time have to leave. But she was always kind to me and made arrangements for me to bathe in solitude, without fear of discovery.

Haji, when he came, called me his desert rat, or his pet jackal, sometimes even his little monster. He was a jovial, large presence, and I couldn't imagine his large, hairy head holding onto a thought for more than a brief moment. He seemed to be always searching out a new entertainment.

We three were together in the middle of the morning a few days later, enjoying a snack of pomegranate juice and roasted almonds. I had not seen Bihzad since our last conversation in the garden.

"Is Bihzad all right?" I asked.

"He has likely withdrawn to his quarters," Maryam told me.

"Is he ill?"

"He has an illness of sorts," Haji said. "It is of the spirit, not the body. It comes upon him and fills him with darkness. At such times he can neither feel the sunshine nor the singing of the birds. It happens from time to time, not often. The company of other people becomes painful to him because his own company is so unbearable. So he withdraws from everyone and everything until the darkness withdraws from him."

"His life here is good," I said. "I understand loneliness, but where is his hardship?"

"You're looking for reason where none exists," Maryam said. "He has the security and leisure to indulge in such moods, so he does."

"What brings him out of the darkness?" I asked.

"I asked him that once," Haji replied. "He said sometimes it's a change in the breeze, or he sees a flower in a new way, or he just wakes up from a deep sleep to find the shadows gone from his mind."

I had another question. "Do others ridicule him for it?"

"Never to his face," Maryam told me. "He is too well respected for that to happen. But behind his back, some think him weak."

"Do you think he is weak?" I asked her.

"Bihzad is his own person," she said, replying without actually answering. "That always takes strength."

"All right!" Haji said, jumping to his feet. "Enough talk. I'm going to drag our friend beyond these walls. The chaos of the city will bring him back to himself. We will wander the streets of Herat until Bihzad leaves his gloom behind and finds his good humor again."

"Take me with you," I said, the words escaping me before any shyness could hold them back. "I saw so little of the city when I arrived, yet it tantalized me. Let me go with you. I'll keep my face covered."

"Of course you can come with us, and your face is perfect. Maryam, what about you? Make your decision and meet us by the big fishpond." He started to go away, then turned back to me and said, "It is very strange that our friend should be waylaid by these terrible moods. When the Sultan is unhappy, Bihzad is the best at cheering him up. He makes a special drawing, and life flows back into the Sultan's face. Why can't he do the same for himself?"

Over his shoulder he called back, "I was not meant to be wise. I was meant to be happy." Off he went to get ready for our excursion.

Bihzad must be feeling that hole that cannot be filled, I thought.

That was certainly something I could understand. Still, Bihzad had two arms and two legs, shelter, food, and a talent that gave his brain something to work on. He had neither physical hardship in his life nor fear in his mind. I could not understand why he was engulfed in darkness when I, who lived with all those things, was not.

Perhaps it had something to do with what he was used to. He had always lived in the colony and had always lived with plenty. For me these treasures were likely to be snatched away at any moment. I could not afford to give the darkness one second of my attention. Back in the desert, it would be free to find me again.

Maryam chose to go back to her ceramics studio. I rushed to get ready.

Within minutes I was out by the fishpond, my face securely covered. Haji may have thought my features were perfect, but, as he said, he was meant for joy, not for wisdom.

Finally Haji reappeared. Bihzad was with him. I'd never seen Bihzad looking particularly robust, but now he looked almost frail, especially beside the well-muscled Haji.

With his big arm around Bihzad's slender shoulders, Haji propelled his friend through the garden, then through the main gate. I followed close behind.

I was so excited! I was about to see the great city without the distraction of an empty belly or the annoyance of an impending execution. My ugliness was securely covered, so I would pass through the streets unnoticed. To top it all off, I was in the company of two people who had shown me kindness, not out of pity, but because they liked me.

I said a prayer of thanks to my mother for keeping me alive, as we left the shelter of the artists' colony and went out into the city.

The quiet garden world of the colony soon gave way to streets and noise and people and life. I stuck close to Bihzad and Haji. I knew from experience how easily the city streets twisted and turned.

"What shall we show our masked friend first?" Haji asked Bihzad. "Queen Gowar Shah's mausoleum? The citadel? The great mosque? The marketplace?"

I was eager to see everything.

"Perhaps another day would be better," Bihzad replied. "I'm very tired today."

"Well, if you're tired, there's only one place to start."

Haji pulled Bihzad down a narrow alley. I trotted behind. After bends and turns too numerous to count, Haji stopped before a wooden door in a brick building looking out onto a public square.

Haji banged on the door hard, with his fist, winking at me as he pounded. Bihzad leaned against the building.

There was no answer. Haji knocked again. "Get out of bed!" he yelled.

A small window in the door slid open. A scowling man peered out. "You're too early. Come back later."

He tried to shut the window again, but Haji put his big hand in the way. "How can we be too early? Is an almond blossom ever early?" He turned his face to me and winked again.

"You are not an almond blossom, you are a man, and a loud, rude man at that."

"It's true," Haji admitted. "I am not someone you would want to grace your shop in the dark of night, let alone in the bright light of the day. However, accompanying me is a man of such refinement and renown, you will soon be cursing me for not banging on your door earlier."

"Oh, and who would that be?"

"None other than Kamal al-Din Bihzad."

The man at the door was stunned into silence. "Not the painter, the great miniaturist?"

"Do you know another?"

"Let me see him."

Haji pulled a reluctant Bihzad over to the window. I heard the sound of the door unlatching.

"Master, you are welcome. I've seen you before, when I made a delivery to the colony. Your work is a treasure for all of Persia. You honor me with your presence."

He gestured for us to go inside.

"We will take a table out here," Haji said. "We want to watch the city."

The shopkeeper seemed flustered. "My staff is not yet here to move furniture."

"Good heavens, man, do you think we are not capable of lifting a table and a couple of stools?" Haji Dost Muhammad's great voice bounced off the walls of the small shop. I followed him in. The scent of ground coffee and other spices almost made me swoon.

In moments we were sitting outside the shop.

"Who is your masked companion?" the shopkeeper asked, bringing cups.

"It could be the Sultan himself," Haji replied. "Treat him as such, and you will be rewarded."

"I am rewarded enough, just by your presence," the shopkeeper said to me, giving me a little bow. It was a nice thing for him to say, whether or not it was true.

He left to make the coffee. I was excited by the prospect of drinking it again.

"We'll take cardamom with it, if you please. No sugar," Haji yelled into the shop. "The shock of the bitterness will do you good," he said to Bihzad.

It didn't matter to me. It was all new and wonderful.

We sat in the shade of an awning and watched the city life in the square. Coffee was brought out, a large urn just for the three of us, along with honeyed almonds and little cakes. Haji poured the coffee.

I breathed in the steam. The aroma was infused with the scent of flowers. "That must be the cardamom," I said.

"It is indeed," said Haji, then he burst out in a great laugh, at my expense.

I had brought the coffee cup up to my mouth to drink, forgetting my face was covered. I'd grown so used to my face being free. Haji noticed, of course, and his laughter drew stares from people in the square.

I could have put the cup down and waited until his attention was elsewhere, but the coffee smelled so good, I had to keep trying. I poked at the cloth wound around my face until I had cleared enough of a space by my mouth for the coffee to go in. Haji kept laughing. I felt so good, with the friendship and the coffee, that I laughed with him.

"It's been a gloomy week at the colony," Haji said, "with our friend here in a sad mood and the Black Pen on a constant rampage."

"I'm afraid the rampage is my fault," I said. "I suggested to the servants that Qalam might learn to appreciate them more if they withheld their services, at least as much as they dare. I gather he has yet to reach the appreciation stage."

"And why did you suggest this?" Haji asked. The laughter in his voice had been replaced by annoyance.

"He hits those who labor for him," I said. "Surely you know this. Why have you allowed it to continue? You are supposed to be the finest minds of Persia."

"Each man's business is each man's business," he said. I got the impression that I was temporarily out of favor as a pet, a hunting dog with his muddy paws on a silk bed cover. I shut down my tongue on the subject.

I looked over at Bihzad. His attention was focused elsewhere, at something across the square.

His fingers reached into the bag he'd slung across his shoulders. He brought out a piece of charcoal and some paper. His eyes moved from the paper to a spot across the square, then back again.

I followed his eyes across the square and saw an old man, huddled against the wall. I looked down at Bihzad's drawing and saw the old man appearing on the paper. I also saw, in the drawing, people walking past him, ignoring him, and I saw the hopelessness in the old man's face.

Bihzad spoke, softly, almost dreamily. "An old man begged at the door of a mosque. He was very poor, and he called for mercy and for alms. One of the worshippers said, 'If you want alms, you should go to a rich man's house. This is not a place where you should expect alms.'

"The beggar said, 'Is it true this is a house of no mercy? How can there be a place where charity does not live within?' The worshipper was outraged. 'Be silent! You profane the house of God!' And he kicked the beggar on his way in to pray.

"From his place on the ground, the beggar could see the beautiful lamps that hung from the ceiling and the elegant prayer areas. He cried out, 'I pity those inside if they have not mercy. I receive alms at every other place I ask. Why should I leave the house of God empty-handed?'

"The beggar stayed at the door of the mosque for nearly a year, without help. Finally, when he was almost dying, a man with a lamp bent over him and offered sustenance. The beggar had the strength left to say, 'I knew if I waited long enough, mercy would come.'"

I recognized the Sufi tale. It was from Saadi's *Bustan.* I didn't think much of it.

"Perhaps I don't understand the way of the Sufi," I said, "but the beggar should have sought help elsewhere."

"It is a story about faith," Bihzad replied, still drawing. "It's about faith in the ultimate goodness of humanity."

I could see that the deadness had gone from Bihzad's face. I glanced at Haji. He could see it too.

"I think it proves the opposite," I said "For a whole year, worshippers ignored this beggar. They were too busy with their pious thoughts to see the need right in front of them. I think it shows that people have a great capacity for seeing only what they want to see."

"Then how do you explain the good man at the end?" Bihzad asked.

This, of course, started off a fine argument. The shopkeeper's staff arrived and carried more tables and benches into the courtyard, setting up hookah pipes and brewing more coffee. More customers came, and they joined in the discussion. Quotations flew between the tables like sunbeams bouncing between mirrors.

"It is rare to find a pilgrim in a coffeehouse."

I looked up from providing a fine point of logic to see the Black Pen standing over us.

Haji pulled over a stool. "Join us for coffee, Qalam. There is still some in the urn."

Qalam remained standing. "Pilgrims lead pious lives, they don't languish in coffeehouses. And those who have taken a vow of silence do not speak."

I waited a moment for Haji or Bihzad to speak up for me, but they remained silent. Very well, I could speak for myself.

"I never claimed such a vow," I said. "I cannot be held responsible for what is inferred by others."

"Where did you come from?"

"My story is for my friends."

He glared at me for a long minute, then said, "Your friends are fools, and if you are their friend, then you must be a fool as well. I wonder how the Vizier will feel, playing host to a pack of fools?"

"Do have some coffee," Haji said. "The brewer here is a true master."

Qalam did not take coffee. He spun away from us with such haste and huffiness that my cup was knocked over and the last drops of coffee in it spilled to the ground.

The three of us sat in awkward silence for a moment. The whole shop had heard the interchange and was silent with us.

It was on the tip of my tongue to say, 'I'll leave, I won't stay to cause you trouble.' But I couldn't say it. I knew the desert was waiting for me, but I was not eager to return to it.

In the end it was a man at the next table who moved the discussion on.

"Herat may be at war again soon," he said.

"Nonsense," Haji retorted. "There has not been a war for many years. We are blessed to live in a time of peace."

"I've heard that rumor too, about the war," another man said. "I've heard it was the Turks on the march."

"The Sultan has good relations with the Turks," Haji told them. "They respect him, and they respect Amir Ali Shah. Why would they go to war with us?"

Amir Ali Shah, as you know, was the oldest friend of Sultan Husayn, and his vizier. A great man, and a good poet.

"It's not the Turks," the first man said. "It's Saybek Khan. He is fighting his way here and aims to capture the city of Herat and eventually all of Persia."

"And yet you sit here, calmly drinking coffee," I said. "A tale grows with the telling."

At that Bihzad and Haji decided they'd had enough of the coffeehouse. Haji paid the bill, and we went back out into the city.

Perhaps it was the coffee that brought Bihzad back to life. Perhaps he felt shame for not speaking up for me to the Black Pen. Whatever the reason, he now wanted to show me everything. We walked from one end of the city to the other, and by the time we returned to the colony, my legs were as sore as they had been after a night's trek in the desert. I relished every step.

We saw the tomb of the great Queen Gowar Shah, whose dedicated to the arts and to learning had brought about the library and colony we lived in and worked in. Haji bought flowers from the merchant nearby, and we laid our show of affection and respect at the blue-tiled tomb.

We saw the Great Mosque with its shining gold dome. Haji and Bihzad went in to pray. I remained outside, under the shade of a grove of apricot trees. I would have liked to join them, but dressed as I was, it would not have been seemly. Which section would I pray in? I enjoyed the sight of the mosque from the outside, and said my prayers in the peace of the garden.

Often when we passed a building, Bihzad would say, "Look at the inscription around that doorway. My teacher, the great Amir Ruhallah Mirak Hiravi, put those words there."

Bihzad and Haji looked closely at the words and engaged in long discussions on the nature and beauty of the calligraphy, conversations I could not follow, nor did they interest me. After the first two times it happened, I took their arms and tugged them gently forward, hoping their attentions would become otherwise engaged before another long, boring conversation overtook them. Usually this worked.

The great sights of the city were indeed wondrous, but my real excitement grew as we walked through the markets.

"Queen Gowar Shah planned all these caravansaries," Bihzad told me. "She was an amazing woman." He swept his arm at the scene before him as he spoke.

Open spaces were balanced with covered walkways, connected by fine roads and passages. We walked under the canopies, where the way was cooler. I saw offices and shops tucked into every corner.

And what shops! Some streets sold only cloth. The streams of silk and linen flowed in every color, down from the ceiling and over the stalls. I felt like I was walking through a rainbow. "This broadcloth comes all the way from England," a merchant said. I was impressed, even though I was not sure where England was.

Other stalls sold jewelry or cosmetics. I saw women there, deciding on pieces of kohl with which to line their eyes and other powders to bring out the color of their cheeks. Men and women looked at the delicacies produced by the gold and silversmiths, and discussed the prices of raw and cut bezoar stones, lapis lazuli, turquoises, and rubies.

I saw smooth, white, round stones I couldn't name, and I asked my companions.

"They are pearls, from Bahrain," Haji told me. "They come from inside a creature who lives on the bottom of the sea. The creature gets a bit of sand in its mouth, and worries over it and worries over it until it becomes a pearl. Divers bring them up from deep in the water."

I could not picture what this creature could look like but thought the job of fetching pearls into the sunshine must be a fine one indeed.

There was a market for tin, one for lead, and one for goods made of iron and copper. The leather market had rough, raw hides for sale and smooth, rubbed, buttery leather fashioned into saddles and shoulder bags. Part of the market sold household goods, and the carpet market was as beautiful as a garden.

"Many carpets are laid out like gardens," Bihzad said. I looked and saw he was right. The patterns and colors of the garden at the artists' colony was repeated in the patterns of many of the carpets.

God can make elephants, and people can make carpets. There is much that is good in the world.

"We Persians love gardens," Haji said. "To us, they are like the promise of paradise. We create them wherever we can, to remind us of what waits for us if we lead a righteous life."

I didn't like him saying that, since I myself had led a life that was the opposite of righteous. I decided I had better enjoy the gardens all I could while I was alive, because after my time was up, a harsher fate awaited me.

The fruit market took me away from such dismal thoughts, with its piles of oranges, walnuts, pistachios, almonds, dates, and pomegranates. The medicine market sold opium ("Good for pain," said Haji, which I already knew from the nomads), strange-smelling herbs, and things like walrus teeth, which Haji had to identify for me, although he could not describe a walrus, and he could not tell me why I might have need of the teeth.

So many images flooded my mind. I have been to many other markets since then—even worked in a few—but that first visit carried with it an excitement never to be repeated.

We got back to the colony as the sun was setting. Both Bihzad and Haji had shoulder bags full of sketches they had done that day. There was no trace of sadness left in Bihzad's face.

"If you ever are overtaken again by melancholy, I read in the library that the boiled hump of a camel will do you a lot of good," I told him.

"It won't do much for the camel," he replied.

CHAPTER FOURTEEN

I began to think that my time at the colony was coming to an end. The Black Pen was not a man to give up, and Haji and Bihzad were not men to fight. They were probably also not men to take such action as to ask me to leave, but that did not mean I would be allowed to stay. Even in my own mind I had overstayed my welcome.

I slept less, read more—against the days ahead when I would have no books—and tried to prepare myself for becoming a solitary wanderer once again.

The night after our adventure in the city, I rose in the small hours of the day and put on my camel-hair cloak for warmth. I left off the winding cloth. The hood and the darkness would hide my face should anyone be around. All was still. The moonlight made the white flowers shine, as if they had their own lantern inside them. I said hello to the fish, then kept walking. My feet took me to Bihzad's studio. I took a lit torch from the hallway and went inside.

The torch did not provide a great light, but it was sufficient. I bent low over the paintings, studying them, trying to memorize every detail so they would live on in my mind once I could no longer see them. The torchlight ringed each painting as I looked at it, but made all the others disappear into darkness. I was able to concentrate fully on each one.

After a time I began to understand what Bihzad had been saying the day he had gotten so upset. The rocks and trees in his paintings seemed to be as alive as his camels and people. His subjects buzzed with energy, as if everything in each painting had something to say.

"I paint what is in my mind," Bihzad had once told me, "not just what is in front of me."

I saw a painting of two people sitting beside a fishpond. I could see in the painting more than I would have seen in real life. When looking at a fishpond, the eye is generally stopped at the surface of the water, unless one is looking straight down into the pond. In that case, the rest of the scene would not be visible.

In Bihzad's painting, I could see everything—the people sitting, the fish in the pond, the snails at the bottom of the pond, the birds in the trees, and rabbits in the grass. It all flowed together. It wasn't realistic, but it made perfect sense.

Another painting showed a man appearing to leap from a balcony. I recognized it as a scene from the *Bustan,* the story of Yusaf and Zulaykha, when Yusaf resists the advances of Potifar's wife. It showed not just the man and the woman and the balcony, but the outside and the inside of the building at the same time. The inside of the building had many rooms and staircases. I counted seven chambers and seven doorways, with connecting steps, cupolas, and carpets, all in a very small painting. It was not a crowded painting either. It was perfectly balanced, and again, it made sense.

"I don't paint just the pond, but the idea of the pond," Bihzad had told me. "The building itself isn't important. We want the idea of the building, the idea of the story."

I was beginning to understand.

"We walk a fine and dangerous line," I remembered Bihzad saying. "Our religion tells us that we who create images will have to answer for those images on the day of resurrection. We do not make our images too lifelike. That would be arrogant. We do not want to imitate the work of God."

As I moved from painting to painting, I began to see why the others were jealous of Bihzad. Their paintings were a little less passionate, a little off-balance. They lacked the grace of Bihzad's, and the mystery, and the wit. Make no mistake—in a million years I could not paint a picture even half as good as the worst painting there. But I began to see why everyone referred to Bihzad as Master.

"What are you doing in here?"

I spun around at the sound of the angry voice, nearly dropping the lantern and sending all the paintings to a fiery grave.

I raised the light to see my inquisitor. It was Muhammad Siyah Qalam, the Black Pen. I turned away, hoping he hadn't seen my face.

"I was simply looking, and admiring," I said.

The Black Pen stepped toward me. He had his own lantern, which he held out before him. "For what purpose?"

"For the purpose of understanding."

"Understanding what?"

Understanding why Bihzad is better at his work than you are at yours, I thought, but was wise enough not to say. "Understanding has value in itself. It needs no further purpose."

"There is something that I wish to understand," Qalam said, stepping forward as I stepped back. "I wish to understand why you keep your face covered."

"It is a private matter," I said, wondering if I could dash past him out of the studio. "I wish to be modest."

"You are not modest of tongue, why be modest of face?" In a swift, solid movement, he knocked the hood back from my head and exposed my face in all its horror. I took pleasure from his recoil, and in that instant lost all my fear.

"You are an abomination," he sputtered. "You are the monster the mob was after, the killer in the desert."

"I am flesh and blood, as human as you."

"You came to this studio to burn these paintings, because you are ugly, with an ugly face, an ugly body, and a soul to match, if a creature like you can have a soul. You hate all that is beautiful because beautiful is what you will never be."

"You are a fool," I said. "The ugliness of how you treat the people who serve you is much worse than the ugliness of my face." I wished I could kill him.

"I don't like being called a fool by something that's no better than the desert it crawled out of. Get out! Leave this colony!"

"I am a guest of Bihzad's and see no reason to leave," I said.

"Either you leave tonight, or you will find yourself in chains by sunrise."

"If you are so sure I am guilty, why let me go free?"

"I am a charitable man," Muhammad Siyah Qalam said, which I doubted. He seemed to me to be the sort of man who would rather eat a starving child than feed it. "But don't mistake charity for weakness. I am not an enemy you want to have."

At that I had to laugh. "I've had enemies all my life, and all are vanquished, never to rise again. You are no more of a danger to me than a fly is to the back end of a camel."

"I will not tolerate such disrespect!"

"You had better get used to is," my mouth said, before my brain could stop it. "Not only are you an insignificant man, you are an insignificant artist. Look around you, fool. What comes from your pen will never match the divine in these."

The Black Pen's face contorted with anger. He raised his hand, striking me with all his fury.

The lantern flew from my hand, landing on one of the rows of paintings. I scrambled up to the rises to retrieve it before the flames could spread. My clumsiness cursed me, my feet caught in my robe, I tripped and clawed my way up. The flames of my lantern had just begun to touch the delicate parchment of a painting. With one hand I flung the lantern into the middle of the bare, stone floor, where it could do no further damage. With the other I slammed it against what was burning, smothering the fire with my flesh.

I returned to the floor and righted the sputtering lantern. I raised the light so that it shone on my burned flesh. I made sure the Black Pen could see and smell it.

"I am stronger than this pain," I said. "You have never imagined that one such as I would come your way."

"What is this?" Maryam appeared in the doorway. She soon had her arm around me.

Maybe it was my voice, maybe it was my face, maybe it was the stench of my wound, maybe it was the witness. Fear flashed onto the

Black Pen's face. He backed away from me and disappeared into the darkness of the hall.

I examined the singed painting. The work itself was not damaged, but the fire had left its mark on the margin.

"Maybe it would be best if I were to leave now," I said.

"Nonsense," said Maryam, "but you should not go back to your hut. Qalam has a bad temper. Stay with me in the pottery studio. I often sleep there anyway."

I allowed her to steer me into the cool of the garden. My hand was beginning to throb.

Maryam fetched salves and remedies. My burned hand soon felt better.

"What would make Qalam act that way?" I asked, not going into the nasty things I had said to him.

"He wants to be the best, and isn't," Maryam said. "He thinks if he pulls Bihzad down, his own reputation will rise. Bihzad brought you into the colony, so destroying you will help to discredit Bihzad."

"But you and Haji have also treated me with kindness."

"Haji could beat Qalam to a pulp," Maryam said, "and even if Haji probably wouldn't, Qalam could never be absolutely certain that he wouldn't. I am just a woman, and in his mind not worthy of any notice."

I helped her repack the box of potions.

"Perhaps you could stay here with me for the next few days," Maryam said, getting out mats for us to sleep on. "There is a lot to do to get ready for the exhibition, and most of my usual helpers have been taken over by the more important artists. I could use your help."

"Of course," I said, grateful and surprised to be asked, to be thought of as useful. "What exhibition?"

"The Sultan has invited all the artists, scholars, and inventors from this colony and others from across Persia to his palace to show our work and join him in a feast. It's an important event, but a lot of work." She added blankets to the mats. "Do you think you can sleep now?"

Even if I couldn't, I settled down and was quiet. It had been an eventful night, and whatever I'd have to face when the sun came up would be easier with some rest.

CHAPTER FIFTEEN

"It is of no consequence," Bihzad said when I showed him the damaged picture. "All my paintings are poor efforts."

Don't start that, I thought. Aloud I said, "Your paintings are masterpieces. I am responsible for this damage. My temper forced the Black Pen to strike me, which sent the lantern through the air."

Bihzad's expression was more confused than usual. "You were struck? There is no striking of anyone in this colony."

"Tell that to my face," I said, but with good humor. "The Black Pen frequently strikes the servants. You've watched him do it. I've seen you."

"Oh, no, no, no, such things don't happen here," Bihzad said. He actually walked away from me.

"I hope you never have to leave here," I called after him. "You wouldn't see evil out in the world until it swallowed and digested you."

He kept walking. I returned to the ceramics studio.

The walls of Maryam's pottery workshop were covered with shelves containing plates, bowls, cups, and vases. They looked exquisite in the morning light.

"We are trying to create fine porcelain like our traders bring back from China," Maryam said. "We have not yet discovered how to do this."

To my untrained eye, the finished pieces that lined the walls were so fine already, I doubted China or even heaven could create anything finer.

"Some of these pieces are from Kashan, where most of Persia's potters work," Maryam said, seeing I'd stopped before a particularly beautiful ewer. It was decorated in different shades of blue, each color ridged into its own shape. Raised portraits of men and women huddled close together, deep in conversation.

"It's like a garden," I said. "Each couple is in their own private section of a garden."

I turned to share my insight with Maryam, but she was busy setting up work for me to do. She placed a mound of clay, covered with a damp cloth, on the workbench. "This needs to be softened," she said, "so that we can add the next element." She uncovered the clay, gave it a couple of pats, and left me to it. She had to mix some glaze to put on a vase she was making.

I prodded the clay with my finger. It didn't move. I didn't think I would be able to do what Maryam asked of me, but I kept at it. The cool clay soothed my burned hand. Gradually the clay warmed and softened. I had to push my weight into it. My shoulders soon ached, but it was a good ache.

I kept expecting the soldiers to arrive to arrest me, as the Black Pen had promised, but as the day went on without that happening, I began to relax. Qalam would be attending the exhibition too. He cared more for his reputation than for my destruction. He could afford to wait and choose his own time.

Pounding and twisting clay frees the mind to think. I wanted to stay and see the exhibition. It would be the crown on the glory of my time in the library. After that I would have no more reason to remain. I decided to be as useful as possible to Maryam and to get myself ready to leave.

A long day of working with clay and being useful in several other small ways restored my spirits. It also got me thinking about how everyone at the colony did something—art, or literature, or astronomy, or mathematics. Everyone was pursuing some kind of vision. Everyone but me. I had no vision, no skills to build upon, nothing to add to the world.

My life had been all about survival. I was beginning to think that survival was not enough. There was also contribution, the joy of seeing a need and then filling that need better than anyone else in the community, perhaps better than anyone else in the world! That was just vanity, of course, but the need to have a point to living is just as strong as the need to stay alive.

I was not nearly graceful enough to handle any but the beginning stages of the ceramics process—Maryam wasn't fool enough to trust me with the finished pieces, and I wasn't fool enough to trust myself. When the time came to pack up for the exhibition, I left the studio so as not to be in the way.

People rushed about all over the colony, getting ready for the exhibition. I imagined Bihzad and Haji would be busy too. I wondered if they would even notice if they never saw me again, then put such thoughts away as unproductive. I was Anubis, jackal of the underworld. I didn't need anybody to miss me.

I took advantage of the chaos to help myself to some dried fruit and a goatskin of drinking water, which I hid away in my hut. The colony was rich, full of things I would need to survive again in the desert. My plan was to gather as much as I could before leaving.

I heard the sound of trumpets and followed their call to the stables. What a sight greeted me there! More than two hundred camels, one for each artist, their saddles draped with flowers and embroideries, were kneeling upon the ground. Each camel was attended to by several handlers, camels being the ornery creatures they are. Behind each camel was a donkey, already packed with the goods the artist was bringing to give the Sultan and display at the exhibition. Adding to the chaos were the drummers and trumpeters and the contingent of soldiers who would accompany the train.

The stable yard was large, but not quite large enough to accommodate all the beasts and people crowded into it. Last-minute remembrances of items forgotten sent servants and artists scurrying to make everything right.

The Black Pen was yelling for servants to get him things, but no one paid any attention. It was a lovely sight.

Haji towered over other men and was engaged in a snorting argument with his camel. Hands on his hips, feet apart, he made a snorty-screechy sound. Then the camel answered him back with the same sound! Haji threw back his head and laughed, then began the dialogue all over again.

"My camel is a much wiser debater than many of the men it has been my displeasure to be bored by in my life," Haji said when he spotted me. "He would make a good civic leader."

"Or a sultan," I joked.

"No disparaging remarks about our leader today," Haji said with mock sternness, "not when he is providing us with this extravagant exhibition. Although it's brought a growl to our wistful friend."

That's when I noticed Bihzad checking the cargo on his donkey. He tightened a few ropes before joining us.

"What do you think of all this, Anubis?" Haji asked me. "We will be parading to the palace in fine style. The Sultan knows how to do things with a flourish."

"He overdoes things," Bihzad said. "Who are we to be celebrated? We are simple people doing our jobs, just like any other servants. Why isn't there a parade of brick-makers, or a parade of latrine cleaners? They deserve to be celebrated more than artists. Their lives are certainly more difficult. And an argument can be made that their work is more necessary."

This from a man who had never cooked his own meal nor cleaned his own latrine, and likely never took notice of those who did.

"Because, O talented but annoying friend, anyone can lay bricks or clean latrines, but not everyone can do what we do," Haji replied. "It is our uniqueness that is celebrated."

"But are we so unique?" Bihzad asked. "I was brought up to this life. I was trained to do this from the time I was a child. How many beggars, bricklayers, and latrine cleaners could do what I do, if only they had the training and the opportunities I have had?"

"Trade places with one of them then, if you feel that way," I said, but with my face covered and the noise in the stables, they could not hear me, or they chose not to, if they had.

"Are you going to grumble all day?" Haji asked Bihzad, pushing him gently in the direction of his camel. "If we are just doing our jobs like any other servants, then, my friend, the exhibition today is part of our job. Our sultan has ordered us to be honored, and we must obey him by accepting it."

I must say now that in some ways I agreed with Bihzad. True, the art I had seen created in the colony was beautiful, but so was the tile work of Queen Gowar Shah's tomb. So were the gardens of the colony. So, too, were the magnificent streets and buildings of the city. They may have been planned by someone who would be celebrated by the Sultan, but the actual carrying and digging were done by people whose names we will never know.

A trumpeter sounded his instrument. Servants bowed before their artists and assisted them onto the camels.

"Hop up behind me, my pet monster," Haji said. "I'm a big man, but my camel is bigger. He can easily bear the weight of us both."

That I could not do. It would feel as if I were pretending to be something I was not. If I had been a bricklayer or a latrine cleaner, perhaps I would have joined him, because my labor would have earned me a spot in the procession. But I had done nothing with my life, created nothing, and contributed nothing except a few more bodies to the desert. I shook my head.

"I will trot along beside you," I said.

Haji wanted to argue, but the camel was getting to its feet. "Make sure you don't lose us," he called down. "I want you sitting on our carpet during the feast. If the entertainment is dull, you can amuse us."

I wasn't sure I liked that remark, but there wasn't time to consider it.

The camels were beginning to move. I got out of their way and covered my face for the journey. As I expected, Bihzad's camel was near the front, just behind the honor guard. In front of the guard were soldiers on horseback, twenty of them, with more moving alongside the camels.

The palace was not a long way from the artists colony. Everyone could have walked there without difficulty, but as I watched the train pass by, I appreciated the Sultan's love of spectacle. Everything was color and excitement. The artists were dressed in their finest clothes. Even the servants had been provided with new attire for the occasion.

I had no fine clothes, of course, but I wore a clean shift and tunic, and flung my camel-hair cloak over my shoulders. The feast would go well into the night and I'd need warmth. My face was covered by a clean winding cloth. I'd managed to find a new way to arrange the cloth, one that left my mouth free to open wide. Maryam had promised me that the Sultan's feast would contain delicacies from around the world, and I meant to try every one of them.

I kept pace with the lead camels. Haji was right behind Bihzad. I think that was more because of Bihzad's friendship than Haji's status in the colony, but I could be wrong about that. Maryam's camel was not far behind. I hung back for a time, looking for the Black Pen. He was riding at around the halfway point.

We turned down a wide street I hadn't seen before, a broad avenue lined with trees and pots of flowers. People from the city had turned out to watch the procession go by. I returned to the front of the train and heard people cheering as they saw Bihzad pass by. Bihzad looked extremely uncomfortable. Haji, of course, was laughing and waving.

I felt both a part of it, and apart from it. I ran up to Haji's camel and put my hand through the saddle strap so I could slip through the palace gates with him.

On the archway above the gates I read the words: The eyes of the world have never before seen an abode so beautiful that it is the envy of the eternal paradise. I wondered if Bihzad's teacher had put those words there.

Inside the courtyard more servants ran forward to assist in the dismounting of the artists and the care of the livestock. The Black Pen's reputation had preceded him. All the servants he called to were busy at other tasks. He had to do his own unloading.

I left Bihzad and Haji to their work and went exploring. There would be many exhibitions for them. For me there was just this one.

An open kitchen had been set up near the stables to feed all the extra servants. Nobody questioned me or paid any attention to me at all. I slaked my hunger there with bread and spiced chickpeas, and my thirst with a mug of *nabidh,* a drink made of fermented dates that the Prophet Muhammad is believed to have loved. Then I went exploring in the palace.

I could describe the palace for you, but you can likely imagine it for yourself. It had all the beauty and splendor that benefits the sultan of Persia. There were gardens within gardens, fountains and streams, tile work of such delicacy and in all the colors of the rainbow. Entrance halls gave way to rooms, staircases to more halls. The artists' colony could fit inside it five times over.

At first it was glamorous and exciting to be able to walk through the palace, then it got to be repetitive. After a while, beautiful things, like beautiful people, all begin to look the same. For variety that will hold your interest, seek out ugliness every time.

I was thinking of going back outside for even more food when trumpet sounds rent the air. The exhibition hall was open!

The Sultan had invited artisans, scientists, and mathematicians from all over Persia and even farther afield. Some worked alone, others in colonies such as ours. Exhibitors came from outside Persia too. Dark-skinned Abyssinians showed their wood carving and needlework, and talked with scientists about their progress in geometry. Arabs came to discuss medicine and physics. Moors talked about architecture. Even those from the Christian world were represented, in bookbinding and biology.

"The sultan believes in learning, and in sharing that knowledge," Bihzad had told me. "It will be a day of celebrating the mind and spirit."

I heard a Yemeni scientist explain how his astrolabe could tell the movements of the planets and thus provide the user with horoscope predictions as well as directions for camel drivers in the middle of the desert.

I listened to an ophthalmologist describe a method that he had perfected for performing surgery on the eye by removing the excess fluid with a special tube he'd invented.

I heard lectures from alchemists and saw the beakers and vials they use to perform their magic with metal.

The mathematicians debated loudly and with much joy on the nature of zero. They challenged one another with number puzzles and had partially completed magic boxes for observers to solve. The right numbers in the right order on the grids all added up to the same sum, no matter in which direction the grid was read. The geometry specialists were there too, as well as explorers of algebra.

Astronomers from the House of Wisdom in Baghdad talked about new stars they had discovered. Others with them showed how they had used an astrolabe to measure the size of the earth.

I saw glass and bronze, brass, and some of the Chinese porcelain

Maryam tried so hard to duplicate. I saw paintings and calligraphy, and sculptures, and combination safes to hold these treasures. My mind and senses were buzzing with all I heard and saw.

I heard Haji before I saw him. His section was crowded, and the crowd was laughing along with him. I hurried over and wormed my way into an opening so I could see.

"It's a clock," Haji was saying. "It tells the passing of the hours and minutes. You could also say it tells the passing of our lives."

He moved the pointers on the dial and an extraordinary thing happened. A little man made of wood came out of the base of the clock and rang a chime, one ring for every hour that the day had reached.

"Do you like it, Anubis?" he asked me after the crowd had moved to another exhibit.

"I have never seen anything like it," I answered truthfully. "It seems to move by itself, but that cannot be possible. You built this?" I was amazed that carefree Haji could create something that required such precision. Perhaps there was more to him than good looks and a ready laugh.

"Come over here. I'll show you how it works."

The clock was carved out of wood and inlaid with polished lapis and other stones. It stood half as tall as I myself, and gleamed softly in the late afternoon light. Haji unlatched a door in the back and showed me a collection of metal and wood parts, moving seemingly of their own volition.

"It's on a spring," Haji said, then showed me his other creations.

There were metal animals that moved on their own ("Same principle as the clock," said Haji) incense burners in the shape of birds, smaller clocks, and boxes with combination locks.

"Why do you bother with paintings when you can also do this?" I asked. "And where are your paintings?"

"Paintings are a higher form of art," he said. "These are just inventions, for fun. The Amir likes me, so he indulges me, or allows me to indulge myself. Paintings are considered a collaboration. Most of them are exhibited together, not under my name."

"Bihzad paints under his own name."

"Bihzad is special."

"Is painting the highest of the art forms?" I asked.

"No, calligraphy is," Haji told me. "A written language is considered to be a gift from God, as is our ability to hold a pen. With these things we can spread the word of Allah and the wisdom of the sages to others."

"But Muhammad Siyah Qalam is a calligrapher, and he was far back from you and Bihzad in the parade."

Haji's eyes twinkled. He leaned into me and whispered. "Mir Ali Shir doesn't like Qalam any more than you do."

"Isn't he a good calligrapher?"

"Technically he's excellent, but his work has no flair, no imagination. You can see nothing of the artist in his work. It's like the man doesn't have a personality."

I could not see how someone's personality could be conveyed in the way he shaped letters and words, but I moved on with my questions.

"You say that painting is considered collaborative—each painter builds on the skills learned by painters around him now and in the past. Isn't all art collaborative…and all science…and all of this?" I asked, gesturing at his creations.

"And?"

"So shouldn't all artists take credit for their work, or none of them?"

"This sounds like the beginning of one of your long, philosophical arguments. Not today, O bloodthirsty creature of the night. Go bother Bihzad. I have admirers to greet." He shooed me away. I left in good humor, not even bothering to correct him. Jackals are no more blood-thirsty than other animals, and certainly a lot less so than humans.

Bihzad was nearby, with other painters. I recognized some from the colony. Others were people I'd never seen before. They sat together on a carpet, their work displayed around them.

Bihzad was discussing his series of paintings showing the army of Tamerlane attacking Urganji, the walled city in Khwarizm. Horses galloped across the pages, their riders, spears and swords drawn, were killing and being killed. I thought briefly of my father's sword, and the things I had done with it, then I put those matters out of my mind and listened to what he was saying.

"If we occasionally extend the paintings beyond the borders, we can enhance their sense of movement and drama, suggesting a greater world beyond the confines of the frame."

In one of his pictures, soldiers in the castle turret rose above the top frame to shoot arrows down on the soldiers below. In another, sword points and flagstaffs broke through the frame's barrier.

"This is not a tool to be used in every painting," Bihzad warned, "as too much repetition will lessen the impact."

"Master," asked one of the listeners, "why have any border at all? Why not paint each painting without restrictions? Why not let each painting determine its own size?"

"If you are painting on the walls of a city or using the desert as your canvas, you may allow yourself such freedoms," Bihzad said. "Here in Persia we illustrate books. We are constrained by the sizes of our books, and for myself, I think that is a good thing. A good painting is as much about leaving out as it is about putting in. We want each work to be our best, and so we must put some thinking and discipline into it."

He went on to talk about how carefully he planned each painting, drawing sketches, thinking about it, even considering which colors would be both harmonious with one another and the eye, and necessary for the story.

A short while after that, the exhibition was brought to a close and we were all called out into the garden for the feast.

CHAPTER SIXTEEN

I felt shy about approaching Haji and Bihzad's carpet. I felt like I was intruding, but Bihzad saw me and came over. His presentation had gone well, and I assumed that was why he looked so happy. I was wrong.

"It's almost over," he said. "Painters should paint. I am honored to be here, for it was the wish of Mir Ali Shir that I attend, but away from our brushes and paints, we are not alive."

"I know you don't believe that," I said. "I have seen you alive and joyful outside of your studio. My guess is that you are not at home among such grandeur and attention."

"What about you, Anubis? What do you think of all this?"

"I like a good meal," I said, "but I've never aspired to it. I can't imagine what work I would do that would be celebrated the way yours is, so I do not yearn for it. I take what life is kind enough to give me and do not mourn for what it does not." Except for my mother. I mourn for her even now.

Bihzad nodded and quoted Khawwas to me. "'Allow what is done for you to be done, and do for yourself what you must.'"

In reply, I quoted Saadi. "'I do not burden another, nor carry another's burden. I do not rule, nor am I ruled. No anxieties—fully I breathe, fully I live life.'"

Bihzad put his arm around my shoulder, resting his hand on my hump. "Come, let us eat now, and drink, and impress the others with our wisdom."

Eat and drink we did, and the glories that surrounded my tongue that night were wondrous indeed. There were goats and oxen roasted on spits, whole lambs stuffed with dried fruits and baked for hours in clay and ashes, eggplant simmered in pomegranate juice, chicken stew cooked by Moroccan chefs in the Moroccan way, and all manner of fruits and exotica from as far as a camel train could travel.

Haji was in fine form that night, replete with jokes and songs. I spotted Maryam on a carpet with women from other nations, talking and laughing and sharing their stories.

The eating continued all night. When our initial appetites had been sated, we were graced by the appearance of Sultan Husayn of Persia and his vizier, the Honorable Mir Ali Shir.

Their presence was announced by trumpeters. We all stood in respect as they approached. We bowed, but as the Sultan stepped onto his raised dais, he spoke. "Please, please, it is I who should bow before all of you. Your work honors all of Persia, and you praise Allah with your creations."

I raised my eyes then, so that I might see these great men.

The Sultan wore a fine robe and had an air of confidence about him. No, it was more than confidence, it was entitlement. He was the highest man in our great land and had no further need to explain himself. I searched his face and saw no signs of cruelty there. He sat quite firmly upon his throne (and would for another eighteen years, although of course none of us knew that then).

Mir Ali Shir interested me more. He was a man of considerable power, perhaps more real power than the Sultan himself, since the Vizier was the one to decide what information would reach his master. Yet he bore very little trace of that power. His robe was simple, like that of a working man. His eyes twinkled, and his face was kind. He reminded me of Bihzad, and of Haji, although Haji had more of a taste for fine things. These good men were forcing me to rewrite my definition of men.

Coffee and hookah pipes were brought out for all, as well as wine and *nabidh*. We ate honeyed almonds and fresh figs as we watched dancers from many regions, heard singers and musicians, and listened to poets.

The great Jami appeared and recited. His poems were brilliant, but he recited as if he knew how brilliant he was and how lacking the rest of us were. I was put off by his manner, and haven't been able to read his work since.

In between each performer, Mawlana Burhan, the great comic, entertained us with jokes and funny stories. Sometimes he pretended to insult people in the crowd. I was glad my face was covered.

The midnight hour had come and gone by the time the festivities finally came to an end. We all stood and stretched ourselves.

Artists and dignitaries came to our carpet to pay their respects to Master Bihzad and extend polite but less effusive greetings to Haji. If they noticed me at all, it was with a puzzled expression, then a dismissal. I didn't mind. I'd had a fine day. Maryam came over to us. We would all walk back to the colony together.

One of the dignitaries was Mir Ali Shir. He smiled and congratulated everyone, looked a long moment at me, then said, still smiling, "If you are here, whoever you are under that cloth, then you are a friend of these good people. You may stay and hear what I have to say. Please keep your demeanors easy, everyone, and prepare to withdraw to my private quarters." Still smiling, he left us alone.

Within a moment we were guided by a servant into a private apartment. We were joined there by Muhammad Siyah Qalam and other senior artists from the colony. I could see that the Black Pen was furious to see me included in the group.

The Vizier soon joined us. "I hope you will forgive my theatrics," he said. "I must speak to you on a matter of secrecy and urgency. I must ask you all to begin preparations to leave your colony and go into hiding in a place some distance from Herat. The possibility of the city being attacked is real. Once the attack happens, we may not be able to spare the soldiers to assist you."

He looked at Maryam. "Your family and the families of the other women will be at the colony in the morning to take you back to your homes. You won't have to travel there alone."

Maryam bowed her head in assent. I could imagine what she was feeling.

"We are your servants," Bihzad said, "but why must we leave? We are artists, not soldiers. We will not be harmed."

"The Sultan believes the artists at the colony—especially you, Bihzad, and the others of high skill—could be kidnapped and taken to Constantinople and made to work for the Turks."

I wondered if that would be such a bad thing. I had seen works produced by the Turks in the colony library, and they showed that the Turks were clearly an accomplished, sophisticated people.

"Is the whole colony to be evacuated?" Haji asked.

"The senior artists are, in small groups, over a brief period of time, Bihzad's group first," the Vizier said. "All efforts will be made to ensure your security and comfort. You will have ample provisions and servants."

"Your efforts are appreciated," Haji said. "I am no desert nomad. I like to be comfortable."

"What of our assistants and the junior artists?" Bihzad asked.

"They will remain behind," the Vizier said. "The colony must appear to be functioning as normal. If there is a mass exodus, word could get back to the Turks. We don't want them to know that we know they may be attacking. We have to assume that there are spies here in the city."

"There is a spy right here in this room," Qalam said, coming forward and grabbing my shoulder. My hump was too rounded for him to grip, and he had to be content with my arm.

"Muhammad Siyah Qalam is stirring up trouble," said Maryam.

"Better to risk trouble than the death of your most esteemed artist, Kamal al-Din Bihzad."

"Then please, speak."

"Bihzad's goodness has clouded his judgment," Qalam said, while I tried to pull from his grasp. "He has brought a stranger into your colony, not caring that there were already accusations of murder against her. This could be the very spy you warn us about!"

With obvious delight, the Black Pen used his rough hands to

unwind the cloth from my face. I tried to be defiant, but felt naked and worthless.

I could not defend myself. I could not explain who I was or where I had come from. I was certainly not a spy, but I was a murderer. There was nothing good that could be said for me.

There was a long moment of silence. We all waited for Bihzad. A word from him would clear me. But he kept his mouth shut.

Maryam was the one who spoke. "Anubis is no spy! I vouch for her absolutely!"

"Master, do you want to take that risk?"

Again there was a pause. Bihzad's silence was deafening to me.

Then the Vizier spoke, to me. "You are blessed with friends, and you have no doubt been a blessing to them. We are Persian, and we are Muslim, which means we are both enlightened and compassionate. The charges against you are serious, and I regret there is no time now to go into their merits. You will be detained here, then moved to a place of more comfortable confinement as soon as it can be organized to do so."

"Master, I'm sure there is no need for this," Haji said, finally but mildly. "Anubis is an amusement, an irrelevance."

The Vizier nodded to his aides to take me into custody.

"This is unbelievable!" Maryam exclaimed. "Master, he who takes advice from a fool..."

"Do not forget that you are just a woman. You would be wise not to complete that thought!"

Qalam spoke again. "Master, you must also consider that this creature has poisoned the minds of Bihzad and his friends. I fear they must also be watched."

"If that is what you fear, then I charge you to be evacuated with them. If you believe they need watching, then you watch them. I am finished with this whole distasteful conversation."

The Vizier left the room. His aides took firm hold of me and began my removal.

"We'll save you!" Haji called after me, mostly, I know, to hear himself say it.

Bihzad remained silent.

And just like that, I became a prisoner.

CHAPTER SEVENTEEN

I did not resist as the Vizier's men took me across the palace grounds, my ugly face shocking the celebrants who remained. I tried to endure the arrest with dignity because—and this is the truth—I did not want to cause embarrassment to my friends.

(The virtue of my stoicism is not diminished by the fact that my escorts were huge and armed and gripped me tightly.)

There was some debate among them about where to take me, and we crossed the grounds more than once, looking for a place that was suitable. Finally they found a stall in the stable that had been used to hold the Sultan's lion, a gift from an Ethiopian dignitary. The lion was long dead and gone, the stall was empty, and into it I went.

"Welcome to your new home," one of the aides said. "Try not to scare the other animals."

They shut the iron door with a bang and walked away. I was left alone on a pile of dirty straw.

My camel-hair cloak gave me warmth and comfort as I tried to calm down and stop myself from shaking.

I counted my blessings—a belly full of wonderful food, a head full of incredible sights and ideas, and as I've said, the warm cloak—but I confess to moments of self-pity and recrimination. If only I had left the palace at the end of the meal! Why did I go with the group into the Vizier's apartment? No one would have missed me if I'd held back. I could have gone back to the colony, gotten my sack of supplies and even added to it, then slipped back out to the cruel, kind desert.

I also tried to feel that my confinement was justified. After all, I had killed. But I couldn't muster up any feelings of shame whatsoever. I didn't deserve much in life, but I also didn't deserve to be in jail.

I was angry at Bihzad and Haji. I was angry at their silence, and I was angry at their cowardice. I didn't expect anything out of life, except that people would be mean, but I had come to think of them as my friends, and friends don't fall silent when their friends are being taken away.

"We'll save you!" Haji had yelled, but I doubted they would. They would get caught up in packing their art and preparing for the journey. If they thought of me at all, they wouldn't for long. Haji had spoken up for me, but I was more of an amusement to him than a friend—a pet, not a person.

I was on my own.

Very well. Things were back to normal.

Except that I was not on my own. Servants came to the stables to get their masters' mounts and saw me there, and the word spread. The finest minds in the nation were soon pushing and shoving to stare at the wonder that was me.

I stood with my head erect, my hideousness uncovered, and did not hide from their eyes. When I could not be provoked with jeers, they took to tossing what they could through the bars. Yet I did not flinch.

In my mind I was back in the garden, having quiet conversations with my friends. I was sitting in the green, cool and sweet, surrounded by kindness and flowers. I was back in the desert, my jackal, Cain, sleeping in my arms. I was in the street of the city, being caressed by an elephant's trunk. I was in Bihzad's studio, looking at his paintings, so delicate and perfect.

And thus the night passed by.

By the time of the sunrise, the gawkers were gone or in bed, and I was left in peace. I curled up on the straw and went to sleep.

No one disturbed me all that day, not even to bring me food or water. I didn't care. I had no intention of staying locked up. A loose stone pried from the wall became my digging tool, and straw covered the evidence. Progress was slow, but steady.

In the end that was not what got me out.

Maryam rescued me.

She came with a key and a bundle in the middle of the second night.

"Are you all right?" she asked, appearing like a happy dream at the iron bars of my cell. She whispered, so I did the same as I rushed up to greet her.

"I'm so glad to see you!"

"I'm sorry it took me so long," she said. "First it was Qalam's guards watching me, then it was my family. I had to sneak away. Come. We must hurry."

We kept to the shadows and ran to the wall at the back of the palace property.

"How did you manage this?" I asked, when we stopped running. She gave me a cloth to wind around my face.

"There are potions for burned hands and potions to put people to sleep. Now I have to put the key back, and you have to disappear."

"What about the others?"

"Bihzad and Haji are leaving the city on a twenty-horse train. They've either left already or they're getting ready to leave."

"And you? What about your work?"

"I may be allowed to return to the studio when this panic is over. I can't give up hope. If my family tries to marry me off, I'll leave. If you can wander the world alone, so can I."

She handed me the bundle and a goatskin of water she had over her shoulder. "I tried to think of what you would need in the desert. Don't go back to the colony. Get as far away from Herat as you can."

I embraced her. "Thank you," I said. There was no time for giving voice to all that was in my heart.

She returned my embrace. "Go," she said. She boosted me over the wall, and I was gone.

I wasn't sure which way to go, then realized it didn't matter. Herat was an island in an ocean of desert. Any direction would take me to the edge. I moved quickly.

I tried to feel defiant, to tell myself that I was glad to be heading back into the desert, that I wanted nothing more to do with these people, these hypocrites who spoke great philosophy but who didn't really care about the suffering of others. I was better than them, stronger than them, and braver than them.

My interior words were lies. I was sad to be leaving a place where I had been treated with kindness and where my brain had feasted with such gluttony.

No matter how hard I tried to hold them back, my winding cloth was soon drenched with tears as I walked through the city, looking for a way out.

Around me, even though the hour was late, there were people in the streets. I could see the fear in their faces. Rumors of war had clearly spread beyond the rich and powerful.

I walked quickly. I was eager to put distance between myself, the chaos, and my pain. We think we can walk away from our pain. We can walk and we can walk, and that keeps us busy for a while, but our pain always finds us again when we pause to catch a breath.

I left that glorious city just as I came into it, under the cover of darkness, and all alone.

CHAPTER EIGHTEEN

I kept walking fast, beyond the city walls, beyond the campfires of the nomads and merchants, out, out into the desert. I walked until my legs ached, until I was surrounded by darkness, sand, and the stars in the sky.

I plopped myself down on the top of a hill and looked back over the city.

I should have felt grateful. I had so much more than I had when I last looked down at the city—a warm cloak, clothes that weren't rags, food, water, a head full of books, the memory of friends. But all I felt was alone, terribly, completely alone.

The problem with being alone is that there is too much time to think. Doubts plagued my head all night, pecking away at my brain like crows pecking at carrion. I should have spoken different words. I should have done different deeds. I knew no peace that first night.

By the time the edge of the sky was tinged with the colors of dawn, I had resigned myself to my newest situation. Not completely, perhaps, but I'd been tossed out of other human communities before. This one was kinder than most. I would spend some time in the desert, wander from hill to hill, stay alive, and go on.

I tried to take my mind back to where I would have been excited to be as well off as I currently was. I knew I could survive alone, because I had done it before.

The problem was, I didn't want to be alone. For a while I was part of something big, as an interloper, certainly, but it was something larger than mere survival.

But mere survival was what I was now stuck with.

The desert is a good place to be when you're in a bad mood or feeling sorry for yourself. It has seen everything, absorbs everything, and is universally unsympathetic. I offered up my loss to the sand and the sky. They received my gift, and in return gave me the promise that the peace of mind I had found there before would one day come again.

I decided to celebrate my improved mood by looking in the bundle Maryam had packed for me. She had planned well for my journey. There was dried fruit, dried meat, bread, and nuts, and an extra shift and tunic, all brought together in a blanket.

I began my journey again, one foot in front of the other. There was something wrong with my sense of direction, because I couldn't seem to make myself go far from the city. I kept the walls within my sight.

I was, of course, waiting for Bihzad.

With so many gates in and out of Herat, there was no reason for optimism, or even hope (which is optimism without foundation). Bihzad could have left already or was at that moment leaving in another direction. I saw other trains, big and small, leaving the city, and I followed each for a time until I could be sure it was made up of strangers.

It was a big desert, but I had nothing else to do. Waiting and watching gave me at least a temporary purpose.

Haji's voice found me before I found him.

I was napping in a rock crevice. The voice invaded my dream and dragged me into consciousness. Before I opened my eyes, I thought I was back in the colony.

My first reaction was to scramble out of my hiding place, follow the voice, and run up saying, "Here I am!" I restrained myself. Instead I crept out, keeping myself flat at the top of the dune so I could look out and not be seen.

I had to laugh to myself at the sight. The Vizier's idea of sending valuable people into hiding was to put them into a train of horses burdened with goods and have the whole thing guarded by soldiers. I was close enough to see Bihzad's face. He was unhappy to be out of his studio. Haji was excited to be on an adventure, safe and protected though the adventure was. The Black Pen looked like his behind was already in pain from the horse. I hoped they had a long journey ahead of them.

I decided to keep my silence, to be their shadow. I was curious to see what they would say around their campfire. Would they talk about me? Would they say how much they missed me? And, like I said, I had nothing else to do.

It became quickly apparent that the guards were of little worth. I followed them for several days, closely enough to hear their talk, smell their cooking, and murder them all in their sleep if I chose to. They never even suspected I was there. Although a watch was posted when they made camp, it was made up of soldiers who would rather sleep than do their duty.

At night the exiles lived like sultans, in tents with carpets laid out by servants, rerolled and remounted on pack horses every morning.

Servants cooked their food, set out their hookahs, and saw to their comfort.

If I was hoping for revealing conversation, wisdom, and insight, I was sorely disappointed. Bihzad was morose, silent, and sulking. The Black Pen complained about everything. Haji spent most of his time taunting the Black Pen.

"Maybe we should leave them all in the desert," I overheard two servants say one morning as they scrubbed the cook pot with sand to rid it of its grease. I was hidden on a ridge overlooking a small valley, where they were camped. The servants had climbed to the top to do their chores in private. If I were them, I would have felt the same. A flicker of loyalty arose in me, but only a flicker. These were men who had abandoned me to my prison. They were accountable for their own behavior.

"How much longer must we put up with this?" the Black Pen shouted, flinging a chewed bone at one of the servants, hitting him square in the chest as they returned to camp.

"I'm sick of your infernal complaining," Haji yelled at him. "There's no end to it. Either shut up or take yourself back to Herat, or the servants and I will kill you and bury you in the desert."

Which made me smile, since the servants clearly wanted to kill Haji too.

"And you, O favored one," Haji said to Bihzad, "if you stopped moping, we might actually enjoy this journey."

Seeing Haji go at Bihzad brightened Qalam visibly. Seeing Qalam happy at his unhappiness brought a fresh volley of bellows from Haji. Their angry, foolish voices rose up from the sand in great waves of ugliness. In the midst of it all, Bihzad, with his long, sad face, looked pathetically comical.

It suddenly struck me that, outside of their cushioned world of praise and poetry, these men were not wise at all.

I'd had enough. There was no more need to shadow them, no more need to sit and wait for them to miss me. I was finished with them, and with that part of my life. Wherever my destiny lay, it was not in their world.

I shouldered my belongings and raised myself. I looked down into the little valley, at my friends and my enemy, saw them all for their flaws and their virtues. In my heart was gratitude, and in my head was freedom.

I was so busy feeling good, I barely noticed when the first soldier was killed.

An arrow flying through the sky found its mark in the soldier's back. He slumped over, without crying out, then slid off his horse into the dirt.

Another arrow caught another guard. Suddenly the air was full of arrows soaring toward the men in the valley like vultures toward carrion.

I didn't think. I dropped my belongings and plunged into the valley, headed straight for Bihzad. By the time I reached him, the campsite was already full of horses and screaming men. I grabbed onto the back of Bihzad's neck and pulled him along so that he was bent double. I'm sure I spoke, perhaps he answered, but the main thing was speed. We ran bent over like that, dodging between horses, the clash of swords like curses in our ears. I didn't know for sure if we were running away from trouble or toward more of it. All around was screaming, running horses, flying arrows, and chaos. I grabbed the reins of a loose horse and we used it for cover.

We ran through the sand and stones and horses' legs. I let the reins fall from my hand, and the horse hurried off in a different direction. We ran into prickly plants and slammed into rocks. We ran blindly, bent with panic. Bihzad may have protested—in fact, I believe he did—but I wouldn't have stopped even if I had clearly heard his objections. We kept moving, my hand so tight on the back of his neck it left bruises.

We made it to the crest of a hill, and I threw Bihzad and myself over the other side. Down, down, down we tumbled, coming to a sudden stop against a rock.

It took us both a moment to catch our breath. Bihzad staggered to his feet.

"I must go. My friends are in trouble."

"You must stay right here and hope the soldiers don't come looking for you."

My words were useless. Bihzad was stumbling back up the hill we had just tumbled down. I got up and followed him.

The noises of battle got louder as we neared the top. I pushed Bihzad down again, and we wiggled to the crest on our bellies.

The sight below was terrible. Bihzad's guard was badly outnumbered. Swords banged, men screamed, horses whinnied and reared up on their hind legs.

"There's Haji," I said, pointing but keeping my arm hidden.

Haji was up on his horse, galloping back into the battle after escaping to the edge of it. His sword was in one hand, waving from side to side but not connecting with anyone. His bellow was louder even than the screams of the dying.

Then he disappeared. I was sure he had been cut down. Bihzad put his face in the dirt, unable to face the thought of harm coming to his friend. I kept watching, unable to look away.

In the next instant, Haji sprang up again! As he broke free from the soldiers, I could see he had hold of something. He was dragging it along beside him as he kicked his horse into a gallop and sped away from the fighting.

"He's all right!" I said, shaking Bihzad. "Look!"

Haji's horse was kicking up a storm of sand as it ran through the valley. A soldier must have realized what was happening, because an arrow caught Haji on his shoulder. We saw Haji droop a little, but he kept riding hard and kept hold of the burden he had picked up from the ground.

"He's got Qalam," Bihzad said, "and he's been hurt. Come." He started to stand up. Did he think an arrow wouldn't strike the Master of Persian Painting? Did he think that because he painted in miniature, he himself was small? I yanked him down again.

"Getting yourself killed will not help your friend. He will tend to his own injuries as best he can. You and I will get to him when it is safe to move."

Neither of us mentioned the Black Pen. We had no way of knowing if he was dead or alive. We would find out when we found out.

We remained crouched behind the ridge.

We heard thunder in the distance, coming closer. It was the thunder of hundreds of horses and camels, their feet pounding on the desert floor, running to help kill a bunch of humans and perhaps be killed themselves.

More troops from both sides joined the battle. The valley below us was full of men and animals. The riders thrust their spears, swung their swords, and let loose their arrows. We could smell their blood and heard the wounded whimpering for their mothers. I was struck again by the thought of how intimate the moment of death is, perhaps the most intimate moment you can share with another person.

"So often this is how I feel," Bihzad said. He had been so quiet, I almost forgot he was there. "So often I feel that I am just an observer of life, that the real work of existence is going on around me, but I sit apart from it, watching. I am not just apart from it, but completely removed from it, behind a hill or a rock or a tree. The world pulsates and grieves and revolves in its turmoil, and I just sit and watch, unmoved."

I was surprised to hear him say that. It was not unlike how I felt, although my separation was in fact, his in spirit.

We said nothing more as we watched the battle. The killing went on so long it ceased to mean anything. The screams no longer hurt my ears, my pity for the dying grew cold, and the sight of blood spilling into the sand prompted no other thoughts than for the feast the vultures and jackals would have.

I took my eyes from the battle and saw a trail of sorts around some rocks and hills. It occurred to me that we should put some distance between ourselves and the killing field, in case the soldiers ran out of enemies and came looking for fresh blood. First, I wanted to get back to the food, water, and warm cloak I had dropped. I pulled Bihzad away with me. It was not easy. He was mesmerized by the sights before us and by his own aching, eternal loneliness. In the end I had to go below him and pull him down by his feet. The posture was not dignified, but it was effective, and we moved away.

CHAPTER NINETEEN

I led Bihzad in the same direction Haji had galloped, hoping to find him. As far as I could tell, he had not been foolish enough to go back into the battle. Even he could be stopped by an arrow.

Bihzad truly had to be led. He seemed unable to move on his own. I was annoyed that he made no remark about me suddenly reappearing in his life. I suppose he was in shock about everything. I thought he would be glad to see me, but better to be sad and alive than dead or captured.

We stuck to sheltered areas as much as possible, pausing only to salvage my bundle. I pushed and pulled Bihzad through rocks and brambles, and rushed him across open areas. The sounds of the battle diminished. At least we were headed in the right direction.

Haji could not have gone far with a wounded shoulder and dragging the Black Pen, dead or alive. I kept my eyes open, looking under each bush and in the shade of each rock. I heard them before I saw them.

The Black Pen was moaning. I heard Haji's voice. "You're not hurt that badly. Stop squealing. Do you want them to find us?"

I pulled Bihzad into the thicket of scrub brushes. For all Haji's bravado, I saw the fear in his face that lasted until he was able to recognize us.

"You're all right!" he exclaimed to Bihzad, rightly seeing him before me, since they were close. Then a proper expression of surprise and joy crossed his face as he saw that I was there too. He tried to rise but winced and fell back to the ground.

I took the water bag off my shoulder, passed it to Bihzad, and dropped to the dirt to look at the wounded men. Muhammad Siyah Qalam had a bad gash on his thigh. I was not surprised he was whimpering. Haji had an arrow still stuck in his shoulder. I wasn't familiar with that type of wound but suspected he was feeling a lot of pain as well.

"You followed us," the Black Pen moaned at me, "you led the enemy to us."

"Shut up," Haji told him, in a voice so loud I almost had to silence him. Once the battle was over, the survivors might come looking for us. I didn't want anyone to spot us—or hear us—unless we spotted them first and had time to get ready for them.

I took the extra shift out of my bundle and tore it into strips with my teeth. Before bandaging Qalam, I took the water bag from him to prevent him from taking any more great gulps of our most precious possession. He swore at me. I ignored him and carefully washed his wound, using as little water as I could manage. Then I bound it with a strip of cloth.

Haji's wound was more difficult. I broke the shaft of the arrow but couldn't pull it out without tearing more of his flesh.

"You'll have to cut it out," he said. He even handed me his knife.

Bihzad held Haji's hands. His shoulder bag had a leather strap, and he put it into Haji's mouth for his friend to bite on. I splashed water on the knife to wash away any sand and cut away enough of Haji's shirt so I could see what I was doing. I hovered the knife over this good man's flesh, unable to cut into it farther.

Then Bihzad started singing. I recognized the Sufi song of praise. It was easy and rhythmic, and he sang it in a low voice, holding Haji's attention with his eyes. When Haji began to hum along, I plunged the knife in. I felt him slump as he passed out from the pain. I had to slice the flesh like I was cutting an orange. I worked quickly but had to dig into the hole I made and grab the arrowhead with my fingers. It was stuck in the muscle. Blood poured over my hand. My fingers curled around the hard point of the arrow and pulled it from Haji's body.

Blood rushed down Haji's back. I poured some more water on the wound. I tore the sleeve off the extra shift in my bundle and used that to pack the wound. "Hold this," I said to the Black Pen. "Do it now," I told him when he didn't move the first time. He brought up his hand. I leaned Haji into Qalam's palm, putting pressure against the wound, then used the rest of the sash to tie it all in place.

I lowered Haji gently to the ground, hoping he would remain oblivious to the pain, but he stirred himself back to wakefulness.

After such exertions, we all needed a moment to pause. I scrubbed at my bloody hands with sand, reluctant to use our little supply of water for washing. It was not an effective way of cleaning. Around me the men were silent, save for the Black Pen's moaning and Haji's labored breathing.

"You don't seem surprised to see me," I said, addressing myself to Bihzad, but Qalam answered.

"Clearly you have been following us, telling the soldiers of our position. We will take you back to Herat in chains!"

Since there were neither chains nor the possibility of Qalam having the strength to move even himself, it was a comment that could be safely ignored.

I waited for a reply, but the next voice was Haji's.

"I know you are not a spy, and I am very glad to see you," he said. "You are a creature of extraordinary bravery and nimble fingers. I believe you are magic, sent to save us and amuse us."

It was a very Haji-like comment, not an insult. I knew his curiosity ended at whatever enhanced his enjoyment of life, and that was that.

I waited still. Haji kicked at his friend. "Our jackal friend here just saved your life. At least say thank you!"

"It is not good to be too attached to anything," was all Bihzad managed to say.

Perhaps he was feeling guilty for not speaking up for me to the Vizier, but I doubted it. I let it go. He'd been raised in the rarefied atmosphere of the Colony, where his talent meant he never had to answer to anybody for anything. Sometimes people just are who they are, and it's foolish to expect anything else.

All the same, I was a little disgusted.

"Where is your horse?" I asked Haji.

"I slapped him on the rear, hoping they would chase the horse and not us."

"A wise move, but an unfortunate one. We could have slung Qalam over its back. Now he will have to walk." I gathered up my things.

"I can't walk!" the Black Pen insisted. "Go and fetch help. I will wait here."

"The smell of blood will draw the vultures, and the vultures will draw the soldiers," I told him. "They may believe you when you tell them who you are, or they may not. How far has your fame spread? They may not even have heard of you."

"Anubis is right," Haji said. "We need to move."

"You can lean on me," Bihzad said. "Between the two of us, we have three good legs."

"But I have shelter here in these bushes," Qalam protested. I could see he was afraid of the pain. I could not blame him for that. He was also afraid of showing his fear. Since he was among friends—friends who didn't like him, but who would do him no harm—that was just foolish.

"'What may appear to be a sanctuary of bushes might also shelter a leopard,'" said Bihzad, quoting Saadi.

"Shut up!" the Black Pen spit. I put my finger to my lips to caution him. "We can't possibly survive out here. Better to be captured. We have no food, no tents, nothing. We've lost everything!"

The words of the great El Gazali came out of the mouth of Bihzad and myself at the same time. "'We possess only what will not be lost in a shipwreck.'" In spite of the difficulty of our situation, we smiled. People are who they are. All the wishing in the world could not make me beautiful.

For the moment I kept silent about my food supply.

"I will go ahead and scout," I said, peering from the bushes. "I can move faster than the rest of you, and the desert and I are old friends."

"You're going to trust our safety to that creature, that spy?"

I turned back and stood firmly over Muhammad Siyah Qalam. "My name is Anubis," I said. "If you do not wish to come with us, then stay here. Someone will likely find you. I hope it's not a bandit."

"Don't talk to me," he said. "Don't you dare even look at me."

"We need to move, and now," Haji said. "What's your decision?"

"I don't have any water," he whimpered. "Leave me with some."

"The water is mine. It stays with me," I said.

In the end he decided to come with us, because, as he put it, he had a duty to the Amir to protect Bihzad and Haji from my treachery. I was relieved, because I couldn't have left him without water, and I had no container to put any in for him. It was a dilemma I didn't have to face.

Qalam managed not to scream as we got him to his feet. He was supported by Haji and Bihzad. I knew Haji was in great pain, but he kept it to himself. Progress was slow, but at least we were moving. I traveled the route three times, heading out to scout, heading back to report, then moving over the ground with the others. Sometimes I went back over where we'd been, to be sure we weren't being followed.

We had to stop every now and then to loosen and then retighten Haji's and Qalam's bandages. This was to keep the wounds from turning black. Things my mother taught me were coming back to me. I saw a plant the nomads had taught me was good for pain, and another that was supposed to help wounds heal. I gathered them and kept them close to me. When we rested, I gave them out. Bihzad and Haji had shoulder bags with them, but they contained only art supplies, nothing that would sustain us. They'd had servants to take care of the mundane.

"Do you know where we are?" Qalam asked. I think he was asking anyone and everyone. None of us knew.

I doled out a few nuts, dried apricots, and pieces of dried goat. We all had another drink of water. Qalam cursed me for keeping control of the food but shut up when I threatened not to give him any.

"Shouldn't we be going toward Herat?"

"I don't know the direction of Herat," I said.

"And we don't know what we would find there," Haji said. "Have the Turks taken over? Who were those soldiers?"

None of us knew. Our lives had not been occupied with military matters. We didn't know uniforms or insignia.

"The attackers could be anybody," Haji said. "No ruler rests easy. Perhaps that is as it should be."

"'Sultans exist to serve and protect their people. People do not exist to serve and protect their sultan,'" Bihzad, quoting Saadi again.

I made us move again. I kept watch while the others slept through the extreme midday heat. We kept moving all that night. Qalam stopped complaining. His leg was bad, and all his energy was needed to face each moment. Haji kept acting like he wasn't in pain—I think he was embarrassed about fainting. Bihzad was quiet, but it was not a tortured quiet. He was bearing a lot of the Black Pen's weight, and that took much of his strength. We were doing all right.

As daylight broke the next day, I saw we were in a valley. Halfway up one of the hills I saw what could be a cave opening. I left the others on the valley floor and went up to investigate.

It *was* a cave, and the climb to get to it was not too arduous. From my new vantage point I could see an easier route up that had not been visible from below. The cave opening was small but sufficient, and there were brambles nearby that could be pulled across to disguise it further.

Cautiously, I went inside. Someone had been there before us but had moved on some time ago. The remains of a cook fire were long cold. The cave was safe.

I got everyone up and inside, then went looking for water. If someone had been there before us, there had to be water nearby.

I found it. It was silty but wet, with no taste of foulness. We were all set.

I gave Haji and Qalam some of the poppy seeds I had found. Chewing them would dull their pain and put them to sleep. There were other things I needed to do, like dig a latrine, scout for food and fuel, but Bihzad insisted I sleep while he kept watch. I couldn't settle at first, so he recited from Hakim Sanai's *Parliament of the Birds* until I relaxed and slipped away.

A few hours of deep sleep is as refreshing as a nighttime of slumber, and I awoke with energy renewed and a deep sense of purpose. There were chores to do, challenges to be met, and I was the only one of us who had the knowledge to meet them. Haji had traveled in the desert, but with an entourage of servants and guards and with camel backs full of provisions.

We were in a kind part of the desert. There were plants we could eat, and I saw signs of birds and animals. Bihzad and I gathered anything nearby that would burn and made a pile near the cave. We didn't have a fire that night, though. I wasn't sure who else was around and didn't know how to hide the flames. The three of us took turns standing watch. Qalam was not well enough to do his share, and the rest of us did not trust him to do it properly.

"I'm happy," Bihzad said when he came out of the cave to relieve me on the ridge.

I looked out over the valley, all light and shadows in the moonlight. I felt the warmth of my camel-hair cloak and the contentment in my belly at having eaten just enough food, no more. I heard Haji snoring behind me, and felt the comfort of Bihzad, flawed but still my friend, beside me.

"So am I," I said. And it was true.

CHAPTER TWENTY

The real work of staying alive began the next day. Three of us—and you can guess which three—approached the challenge with joy and excitement. The fourth remained on his back on the ground.

Of course the Black Pen could not walk around, but he could have put his hands and mind to use instead of using all his energy to moan and call for more pain medicine. Some people look for joy. Some people look for misery. Each one tends to find what they look for.

"You are the expert, Anubis," Haji and Bihzad told me. "You tell us what you want us to do."

I enjoyed telling the greatest of all living Persian painters how and where to dig the latrines. Bihzad dug a separate, private one for me and decorated it with desert flowers, which was unnecessary but kind.

Haji solved our problems. We needed clean water, a safe way to build a fire, and a way to take care of Qalam's personal needs so that they did not pollute the cave. (He could have crawled out to the latrine, but he was Qalam.) The desert is full of things that can be made into other things, if only the traveler has enough vision and enough need.

Haji took on each task and was successful. He built a screen to go around the fire to shield it from passing eyes. With much aching and sweating, I finally managed to get a fire started using sticks and tinder. We nursed it gently until it was established and kept it going even in the heat of the day. The screen reflected the fire's heat back into the cave at night. It was needed, particularly by Qalam. Unable to move around much to get warm, he felt the cold worse than the rest of us.

Bihzad kept track of the meager supply of food I'd brought. I remembered what the nomads had taught me and added to it when I could. Almost anything tastes good when you roast it in a fire.

"I've made us some torches," Haji said. He showed off his new creations of grasses wound tightly around large sticks. "They won't burn for long, but we can use them to explore the end of the cave."

Our cave, as we had discovered, went far back into the hill. The cavern near the opening, where we stayed, received a bit of light during the day. Behind us, the cave was in total darkness. We knew there were no people or lions back there, because we would have heard them, but that was all we knew.

"Where are you going?" Qalam demanded to know when he saw the three of us, each carrying a torch.

"We are going exploring," Haji said cheerfully. "We will not be gone for long."

"You can't all leave me!" Qalam yelled. "What if some misfortune befalls all of you? What will happen to me?"

"You will die soon after we do, and we will all meet up on the other side." The cheeriness in Haji's voice was unmistakable, not at the prospect of the death of us all, but at the prospect of exploring the cave.

The start of a new journey, big or small, is always exciting, even if the journey turns out to be dull or disastrous.

We left Qalam to his complaining. I touched a red ember to the grass on Haji's torch. It sprang into light. Haji led the way, and we went deeper into the cave.

It was clear that people had lived there long ago, and died too, as we saw several collections of bones. Bihzad found pieces of pottery, but nothing whole that could be useful to us.

"Who do you think they were?" I asked.

"Nomads, exiles, hermits, criminals—the desert of Persia has seen them all," Haji said.

His torch was beginning to fade. Bihzad touched the tip of his to the remains of Haji's, and we had bright light again.

Bihzad was the first to spot the drawings. He held the torch up to the wall, and we all stopped breathing.

The wall was full of art.

"There's a horse," Haji said, "and a camel."

"Some of these tell the story of a hunt," Bihzad said, reading the pictures the way some would read a book. "Others tell about a trip down a river." I saw a person sitting in a boat. I saw trees, and something that could be a lion, and a drawing that looked like two people trying to kill each other.

"All through time, we humans have needed to draw," Bihzad said. "We have needed to use our hands and eyes to try to understand what is happening around us. We have needed to say to the future, 'I was here! I was alive!'"

"Do you think the people who did these drawings were concerned about the future?" Haji asked. "Could they even conceive of the future?

Can we?"

His last question was particularly wise, I thought. We can conceive of the immediate future, perhaps twenty years hence, but can we imagine a hundred? Can any of us really imagine the world existing after we have passed on? We know that the world continues to exist after other people die, but how could it exist without us? Time should stop and all should go dark. All right, perhaps we can conceive of other lives continuing after our own has ended, but it is not a pleasant thought. We gain strength from pretending that we and we alone are the reason for the universe. Without that notion, our unimportance is too overwhelming.

We stared at the paintings until Bihzad's torch was gone and mine had nearly burned out. We made our way back to the outer cave in darkness, feeling the sides of the walls and tripping over rocks and bones.

"Where have you been all this time?" the Black Pen asked. He knew where we had been. He was really asking how we dared to leave him for so long.

"We have been gazing at immortality," Haji said. His voice was full of reverence for what we had seen.

"The only immortality comes from close friendship with the Sultan, which I have and you haven't. I am feeling very bad. You must have done something to make me feel this bad."

Haji did his best to see to Qalam's needs. I actually felt pity at that moment for the Black Pen. He believed such foolish notions. Of all the many things that are real and lasting in this world, rulers are the flimsiest of all.

Overnight, Muhammad Siyah Qalam took a turn for the worst.

"His leg is going sour," I said when I took the bandage off the next day. The announcement was unnecessary. We could all smell it.

The sourness had moved into the rest of his body. His skin was hot to touch, and clammy.

"He could die," Haji said. The Black Pen was no longer responding to us, not even to complain. He was lost in a haze of pain and vagueness. "What can we do?"

I searched my memory. There must be something that I'd read or seen that would save him. I didn't like him, but he was so sure I would kill him, I didn't want to give him the satisfaction of being right.

"We need to cut the poison out," I said with more certainty than I felt. "He will need to drink a lot of water to push the poison from the rest of his body. And we will need to keep him warm, so he can sweat it out."

The pain would be terrible. Bihzad built up the fire with reeds and sticks, and Haji heated his knife in the flames. We decided that Haji would hit Qalam on the head first, to knock him out and keep him from feeling anything.

"How will I know how hard to hit him?" Haji asked. Neither Bihzad nor I knew. Haji shrugged, raised the rock with his good arm, and brought it down on the head of the Black Pen. Qalam head lolled to one side, but he was still alive.

I worked quickly, helped by the hot knife. It was an unpleasant job, made worse by not knowing for sure if I was doing good or causing more harm. The stench was horrible. We bound the clean wound, covered Qalam in layers, and hoped for the best. Haji scraped up the soiled sand and took it outside to bury.

All through the long day and night we bathed Qalam's forehead, poured water into his mouth, and looked after his needs. Haji had rigged up a filtering device to take the silt out of the water, and Bihzad went back and forth to the water supply, keeping the goatskin filled. I brewed tea by putting hot rocks into a leather pouch of water, using any leaves and roots I found that I knew not to be poisonous. I crushed seeds from the pain-numbing plant and put the paste between his lips. I knew the taste was bitter, but the Black Pen was in no position to argue.

By dawn the next day Qalam's fever had broken, and by midday he was complaining. His recovery was steady after that, and we could all get back to the pleasure of disliking him.

"When are we leaving here?" he grumbled. "You have no right to keep me here."

"We'll leave when you are well enough to travel," Bihzad said, and I got the impression he was in no hurry for that to happen.

"If you don't like it here, you are free to go." Haji, whose own wound was healing nicely, had no more patience for the Black Pen.

I found the den of a desert hare, complete with a nest of babies. The young rabbits would have gone further in a stew, but we had no cooking pot. We roasted them in their skins over the fire, to keep all the fat in, and their little bodies made us all feel stronger.

"Why don't you like me?" I asked the Black Pen when I brought him his portion of food.

"I, too, am interested in your answer," Haji said. "Anubis is not an artist, so she is not in competition with you. She has not spoken ill of you to those in high places. In fact, her existence has nothing whatso-ever to do with you. So why do you dislike her?"

Bihzad was tending to the fire, adding just enough fuel so that it would not go out and force us into the ordeal of restarting it. He added one last stick, then sat beside Qalam. He said nothing, just waited for him to answer.

For a long time Qalam refused to speak. Then he said, "Because she is nothing, and she believes she is our equal. Because she is ugly, and therefore sinful. Anyone that ugly is being punished for something."

"I was born this way," I said. "What crime could I have committed before my first breath?"

"How could I possibly know that?" Qalam said, rising up on his elbows in anger. "Perhaps the crime was done by your ancestors, or perhaps your face was arranged this way by Allah, as a warning to others to stay away from you. Do you think that I would be so arrogant as to question the intentions of the Creator?" The outburst had taken a lot of energy, and he lay back down.

"I don't think so," said Bihzad slowly. "I think you despise her for much baser reasons."

Bihzad went back to the fireside and took pen and drawing paper from his bag. With his back to Qalam, he began to draw.

Again the Black Pen wouldn't respond.

I grew bored waiting for something I didn't really care about anyway, and went outside.

The heat of the day was intense, and I kept to the shade. We were comfortable in our little cave, and safe. Our watches now were sporadic. Even so, no one bothered us. I could have used the time to come up with a plan for our future travels, but it was too hot to think. I looked out across the vast, remarkable plains of Persia and thought about the Black Pen's words.

Of course he spoke nonsense, foolishness from a foolish, mean mind. But I was a criminal. I was a murderer. Along with all the other things I was, and might one day become, I was also a murderer. I looked down at my hands. Bits of Haji's and Qalam's blood were still there, around my fingernails. I thought of other blood that had flowed on my hands, that I had caused to flow.

I sat quietly with my thoughts for a long time, and kept them with me while I went about my camp chores.

When darkness fell, I gave the Black Pen some more pain-killing poppy seeds to chew, and joined Haji and Bihzad around the fire. The flames were low, the smoke was sweet, and the embers red and warm. I spoke into the quiet of the night.

"There are things about me I now wish to share with you," I said. I realized then that I didn't share them before because I thought my friends to be without flaws. Now that I had seen their imperfections, and still called these men my friends, I wanted them to know me.

"I killed five men," I said, speaking without fear. "I killed them when they were asleep and could not fight back."

The fire sputtered at a knot in a piece of wood and sent sparks into the air.

"Tell us," Haji said. There was kindness in his voice.

"I am from Mashad," I said. I told them my father's name, although it would mean nothing to them. "He ordered me taken into the desert when I was born. He condemned me to death, but I defied him even then and survived. My mother and the other wives raised me in secret. When my father killed my mother in a fit of brutality, I killed him with his own sword. Then I took to the desert.

"In the desert I came upon men who were drunk on wine and on their power over the woman they had brought with them. I could hear her screams. When the wine sent them into sleep, I crept into their camp and ran them through with my father's sword. I meant to rescue the woman, but it was too late. They had already killed her. I left one man alive, to show him the horror of my face and deed. Word got around. For a long time the legend helped me survive.

"But legends only go so far. I came to your colony escaping execution. I came out of the desert with an empty belly and encountered people of the city. They hadn't heard the stories, so when I tried to steal their food, they saw me only as a thief, and an ugly thief at that. And then one of their number turned out to be the man I'd left alive. My death became their sport."

I ran out of words then, so fell silent and looked at the fire. I used a long stick to poke a straying bit of wood back into the heat.

"Are you sorry you killed?" Bihzad asked. His voice was almost a whisper, and I could not read its tone.

"I'm not sorry I killed my father," I said. I wasn't then, and I'm not now.

"What about the men in the desert?" Haji asked. "Are you sorry you killed them?"

"I am," I replied. "They had stolen and killed a woman, so their lives were not worth anything to me or to any other woman, but I didn't know everything I should know." I struggled a bit to bring to the surface thoughts I hadn't fully known I was carrying around. "I didn't know them. They were nothing to me. Killing someone you don't know is too easy to do without thinking about it. Killing should never be easy."

"What about the woman the men had stolen and killed? Would you kill to protect her?"

"She was already dead by the time I got down to them. I heard her screaming, but I did not attempt to rescue her. I don't know that I could have done anything, but now I wish I had tried. The legends about me are bigger than the truth, but at least I might have been able to escape hell."

"You believe you are going to hell?"

"I know it," I said, "and it doesn't frighten me. I've seen how horrible the creatures of the Earth can be. Can the creatures of the underworld be any worse?"

We were all quiet for a long while. Then Haji said, "You have acted, where I have only pretended to like action. You have stood for something, where I have only stood for looking like I stood for something. Dragging Qalam off the battlefield was the one true act of bravery I have ever done in my life, and I know I will build it into a tale of monumental heroics when we get back to the coffee shops of the city. I fear I will spend my old age warming myself in the sun and wishing I had been more like you."

"Do not wish that," I said. "Killing is nothing. It takes no bravery or intelligence, especially not the way I killed."

"But you took a risk," Bihzad said. "You risked being found out and killed in return. I do not risk so much as a voice raised in polite opposition when a friend I know to be good is taken away as a prisoner."

There was nothing I could say to that, so I said nothing, although I was glad that Bihzad knew about his silence and bore the pain of it. He may be a great painter, but he had a lot to learn about being a good friend.

We left our thoughts to the night. Soon after, Haji and I went into the cave to rest. Bihzad stayed on watch, although there was little need for it.

Before going to sleep I checked on the Black Pen, in case he needed more poppy seeds.

"I knew you were a criminal," he said. "I will see that you meet up with justice."

I put the pouch of seeds away, and left him to his misery.

CHAPTER TWENTY-ONE

My mask had been stripped away.

It was one thing to carry my crimes with me in my heart and head. I could not hide my physical ugliness, but the deformities of my soul were private. I could hide them beneath my intelligence and my self-possession. Not anymore. My flaws were out in the bright light of day, available for all to see.

Strangely, though, I didn't mind that. The burdens of my soul were my own to carry, and carry them I have, all of my long life. Whatever I meet up with after my death will be mine to face. But I had no secrets left. I was who I was, I had done what I had done, and the end of secrecy meant the end of shame. I felt ready for whatever would come next.

Haji got Qalam up and walking the next day. The Black Pen was able to put some weight on his leg and talked about getting back to Herat.

"Herat is a big city. It can't be that difficult to find." Clearly he had no previous experience in the desert, where it is much easier to be lost than found.

Bihzad and Haji were in no hurry. "What awaits us back in Herat? If Sultan Husayn sits firm on his throne, we will soon be back at our easels and workbenches. If there is a new ruler, there will be some confusion, but we will soon end up back where we started, with our work, surrounded by what we know. Let's live with the unfamiliar awhile longer."

"You know that when we return, your ugly friend will be arrested for murder, and executed. You want to deny me the glory of seeing justice done."

"Off you go, then," Haji said. "I'm happy here."

"As am I," Bihzad said.

Bihzad had his work with him. He looked as at home in the cave as he had in the garden of the colony or in his art studio.

"I have worked out the answer to the question you asked of Muhammad Siyah Qalam," he said, showing his work to Haji and me. It was a drawing of several men in beautiful robes, holding a discussion in a courtyard garden. I looked hard but did not understand.

"It is called *A Meeting of Scientists,*" Bihzad said, which still didn't tell me anything. He explained further. "In the center of the courtyard are men of great learning from all the great centers of culture and serious study. They have spent years gathering and perfecting their knowledge. They have received honors and decorations, and are recognized as men of value and importance."

He pointed to a ragged-looking man standing apart from the main group. "This poor man doesn't belong. He is just as wise as the others, and even wiser than some, but he is not one of them. He is a beggar who was just passing by, heard the conversation of the important people, and joined in. But the learned men, scientists, theologians, writers, and artists do not listen to him. How can someone so poor, so unimportant, have anything to say that *they* would want to hear? They are part of the royal court! Everyone recognizes their greatness! If this intruder, filthy, smelly, poorer than a dog, is given any credence by these great men, it will make them question whether they are truly as great as they think they are."

I looked again at the picture he had drawn. Even without the colors added, the details were clear—the expressions of disdain on the faces, the postures of exclusion. I looked especially closely at the man on the outside.

"He doesn't seem bothered that they won't acknowledge him," I said. "There is no longing in his face, or shame."

"That's because he knows who he is," Haji said. "He doesn't need his wisdom or his talent confirmed by people who think they are important. He is complete in himself."

"He is equally comfortable with knowing what he knows and knowing what he doesn't know," Bihzad added. "He is someone to be admired, but who will not understand or care about the admiration of others."

"Will he ever be accepted?" I asked, but I already knew the answer.

"He will not," Bihzad said. "When someone in the group of important people finally realizes the strength of the stranger's thoughts and ideas, he will offer the stranger an honor in the form of a large, fine turban so that he may sit with the others as an equal."

"The stranger turns it down," Haji said, knowing where Bihzad was going. "He doesn't need it and sees nothing to gain from remaining in the company of those who do."

"What happens to him?" I asked, thinking I knew, but afraid to have it confirmed.

"He will move through his life, contributing his wisdom and gathering more, and the world will be better for his having lived."

But alone, I thought. He will move through his life alone.

"At least you didn't make him ugly," I said, trying to joke.

"That's because *you* are not ugly."

At that I wept, and was embraced by my friends, and when my feelings grew too intense for me to understand, I went out alone into the desert, which understands everything.

CHAPTER TWENTY-TWO

This part of my story really ends here.

There were a few more weeks in the cave, and the journey back toward Herat, but the next page in my life had already turned. I knew for certain that I would not return with them to the library—*not* out of fear of arrest—but I didn't know what would come next. I was between lives, which is not an unpleasant place to be if, like me, you lack expectations and are prepared to deal with whatever comes next.

When they weren't taking care of the most annoying Black Pen, Haji and Bihzad worked on their own projects.

Haji made use of all sorts of things he found in the desert and in the cave. He created things he called sculptures that reminded me of his clock. The one I liked most had a series of ramps and pulleys. Everything that happened caused a reaction somewhere else.

"I'll leave this here when we leave," he said. I was grateful for that. His creations were huge, and I didn't know how we would move them across the desert with us. "The people who come here after us will have such fun discovering them and wondering what sort of people could have created them."

I asked him if he would make other things like them when he got back to his studio.

"Maybe in my spare time," he said, "for my own amusement. They have no real value."

I was saddened by his answer. I thought his sculptures had a lot of value, and they gave him such joy. Haji was a good painter, but not an inspired one. If he stuck to painting, he would always be second-rate, far down the line in abilities from Bihzad. His sculptures would set him apart, but it was not my decision to make. It struck me as odd, though, that someone so bold and life embracing did not have enough courage to go his own way.

Bihzad made pages and pages of careful drawings. He drew a lot of battle scenes. I saw a new figure drawn into each one—a man alone, with a sad face, watching the battle from the top of a hill or from behind a rock. He looked lonely, perplexed, almost a different creature altogether from the ones he was watching.

I knew that this was how he saw himself, and I think it did him good to paint himself like that. We are what we are, and to be able to see ourselves clearly keeps us from wasting a lot of time.

The Black Pen kept up his threats. "The rulers of Mashad will pay a great price to know who killed your father," he said. "You must be glad to know that your worthless life will be turned into gold coins for my pocket."

His words didn't bother me, because they had no power. I didn't care that he didn't like me. My life was full without his affection. He had no power to carry out his threats, and my desert wisdom was greater than his. I knew I'd be all right.

Haji got Qalam up and walking. Qalam squawked the whole time, but he got stronger with each try.

We were eating, but not much, and the water supply was getting siltier all the time, until in the end it was more silt than water. Every day I walked several hours in one direction and then another, looking for food, better water, fuel, and some sense of where we were.

It was time to think about moving on.

I don't know what we would have done if the tribe of nomads hadn't wandered into the valley below our cave.

They arrived there late one afternoon. After warning Qalam to keep quiet, Bihzad, Haji, and I crept down the hill to where we could hear their voices. We listened to their conversations. I recognized their language and thought I'd be able to recall enough of it to be able to ask them for help.

Haji and Bihzad and I approached them in the full light of the morning. I kept my face covered. After exchanging plenty of respectful greetings and giving them time to look us over, I stated our business.

"We are four travelers from Herat. We have fallen on misfortune and ended up in the cave above you. We are looking for guidance to get us home."

"If you are looking for guidance, pray to God," a man said, not wanting to be too helpful too soon.

"We turn to God with our praise and our joy," said Bihzad. "For help we turn to you, so that we might all use the talents we've been given."

On it went, for some time. The nomads were not traveling that day, so the men had time to play games with us. The women were always working.

Haji had an idea. He and Bihzad went back up the hill to fetch one of his sculptures from the cave. While they were gone, one of the men asked me why my face was covered.

"You are not this desert monster we've heard about, are you, the one that kills and eats its victims? We heard it keeps its face covered, just as you do yours."

"I am not," I said, "and don't believe anything you hear. I keep my face covered because it was burned by a rolling piece of wood from a cooking fire when I was very young. Even now the sun makes the scars hurt." I was through with the legend. I didn't need it anymore, and didn't want to go back to using it, no matter what happened.

Haji and Bihzad got one of the moving sculptures down the hill and into the nomad's camp. The nomads were a little afraid of it at first, then laughed and had fun with it.

They knew where Herat was. They were not planning to go there, but they promised to take us within sight of the Hari River. We could then follow the river all the way into the city.

We took them to see the cave and to meet the Black Pen. He scowled at them, and they made up insulting jokes about him in a language he couldn't understand. I shared the insults with Haji and Bihzad, and we all had a good laugh, even though Bihzad looked a little ashamed of himself for laughing.

What more is there to tell?

We left the next day. Bihzad and I helped with the chores, and Haji carried the children around on his great, wide shoulders. I was pleased at how well his wound had healed.

After three days of walking we could see the river. The nomads left us there. They were going on to high pastureland.

No payment was expected—this was desert hospitality—but Haji wrote them a letter they could not read.

"The next time you are in Herat, come to the place written here. Ask someone. They will help you find it. You will be our guests for a feast."

It was a friendly gesture, but I doubted the nomads would do it. Haji didn't understand that there were people who didn't think in terms of words on a page, who could not think that symbolically because their lives were too full of harsh realities. They hadn't time for such extravagances. But we were such strange company—Bihzad with his drawings, Haji with his great laugh and his bizarre creations, me with my covered face, and the Black Pen with his lame leg and growly words—that we gave them enough material for many nights of story-telling. Not a bad gift at all.

We camped that night by the river. There were boatmen to sell us fish. Qalam had some money, which we forced him to part with. There was river water to drink and enough dry stuff around to make a fire.

"Soon you will be executed," the Black Pen said to me. "How does it make you feel to be so near to death? Do you hear the creatures of the underworld calling to you in your sleep?"

"That's enough!" Bihzad said, rising to his feet and actually raising his voice. "You go on and on about turning Anubis over to the authorities. You talk with such glee about seeing her executed. If you want her death so much, why make others kill her? Kill her yourself, right here, right now."

He grabbed a piece of wood from the pile by the fire, and thrust it at Muhammad Siyah Qalam. The Black Pen was frozen still. He made no move to accept the challenge, and held his tongue after that.

We didn't talk deeply that last night together. We had already said everything we had to say to one another. Mostly we sang Sufi songs and made up humorous versions of the arrogant Jami's poetry. It was a good evening, sad and happy. We were all feeling eager to get on with the next part of our lives, whatever that would be. For myself, I still didn't know.

I thought about sneaking away during the night so that I wouldn't have to say good-bye, but I slept heavily to the peaceful sound of the river flowing. The sun was well up by the time I opened my eyes.

The others were awake and ready.

"I've found a boatman to take us into Herat," Haji said. "He says all is well there. The battle we saw is all there was of the war."

The boatman was ready to leave. Haji and Bihzad were anxious not to keep him waiting. The Black Pen was already on board the boat, his back to me.

"I won't say good-bye, my little jackal," Haji said to me. "It would be a lie, because I know we will see each other again." We clasped hands. I felt his strength and remembered his humor, and thanked God for this good man. He stepped aside, and Bihzad stepped forward.

Even now that I am very old I cannot bear to think about that parting. It was like parting from my mother, all over again.

Neither of us was able to speak. He handed me a rolled-up piece of paper, embraced me and held me close, then turned and walked quickly to the boat.

I never saw Bihzad again.

I sat on the shore for some time after they left, not sure what to do next, and not really caring.

Late in the afternoon a fishing boat stopped and tied up nearby.

"You there," a man on the boat called out. "Are you looking for work?"

"I suppose I am," I replied.

"Ever work on a boat?"

"No, but I can learn."

"Why is your face covered that way? Do you have the plague?"

"No, I'm healthy, just ugly."

"As long as you don't scare the fish away."

That was the extent of my job interview. I learned the fishing boat business, and learned it so well that by the time they discovered I was a woman, I was too indispensable for them to care.

It was three days before I could unroll the paper Bihzad gave me. It was, as I suspected, the drawing of *A Meeting of Scientists*. He told me in the cave that he'd make a painting of it when he got back to the studio. I hope he did. I hope he remembered me.

I've lived many lives since then. I got tired of fishing and met someone who needed an elephant keeper. When I found out he was planning to sell the elephants to an army so that they could be used in battles, I stole them. The elephants and I spent five years hiding in the wilderness until I could get them safely into India.

I kept traveling. I saw India and much of China, and I took notes on everything. I even drew a few pictures, but they were quite terrible.

I made it to Europe. I wandered into Germany, wanting to look at clocks, but got out again quickly. German priests were on a witch hunt. Anyone who looked or behaved a little differently from the usual ended up roasting on a stake. If the Prophet Jesus were around today to see what was being done in his name, he would become a Muslim.

In Italy I made a lot of money exhibiting myself as a curiosity.

People paid to see strange things. I called myself the "Ugliest Woman in the World" and traveled with Petrus Gonsalvus, the dog-boy from the Canary Islands. The money was pleasant, but the work was unsatisfying. I already knew that most people are idiots, and so learned nothing new.

In Rome I made friends with a man who was painting the ceiling of a large chapel. His canvas was big, while Bihzad's was small, but their struggles were the same. He and I would sit in the empty chapel late at night, drinking wine. I told him stories of the desert, and he complained about his pope.

I've led a long and varied life. I've been set upon by enemies and welcomed by friends. I've been discarded by my father and loved by my mother. I've killed men and saved their lives, been spat upon and been beloved, seen the worse of ignorance and the best of wisdom. Not everybody can say that.

Bihzad, Haji, and Maryam showed me how kind people can be. They taught me that there were things about me that others would like, and treated me with the respect I have since expected from everyone else I've chosen to spend time with. I've missed them, but I carry them with me.

I *did* see Haji again, quite by chance. He was in jail in Khartoum. I almost landed in there myself, breaking him out. But that's another story.

Bihzad's Life and Work

Not much is known for sure about Bihzad, the man. Details of his life are sketchy.

We know he lost his parents when he was very young, possibly to plague or other disease. He was raised by Amir Ruhallah Mirak Hiravi, who was such a celebrated calligrapher that his work was allowed to appear around doorways of many of the greatest public buildings and palaces of the time. Mirak became the head librarian in Herat, and it is likely that this library, or complex of libraries and art studios, was where Bihzad grew up.

Bihzad came of age at a time and in a place that was a hotbed for thinkers and creators. Bihzad was surrounded by such artistic giants as painter and inventor Haji Dost Muhammad, calligrapher Sultan Ali Mashhadi, painter Shah Muzaffer, the poet Jami, and Bihzad's teacher, Mawlana Wali Allah. It was a time when the Islamic world bubbled over with scientists, philosophers, mathematicians, and others on the cutting edge of intellectual explorations.

The rulers of the day, Sultan Husayn and his treasurer, Mir Ali Shir, loved the arts and funded artists, building them places to live and work, and giving them the protection of the state. The price of this support and protection was that the artists were not free agents, able to paint what they wanted. Although the patronage was a benevolent one, it did create conflict within some of the artists, including Bihzad.

Bihzad belonged to the Naqshbandi order of Sufis, as did Jami and Mir Ali Shir. Sufism celebrated the possibility of personal union with God while still in this life. Some Sufis lived as mystics in the desert; others were itinerant preachers, living off the alms of the faithful. Still others were dervishes who sang praises and whirled in dances of ecstasy.

Bihzad cared little for worldly goods. He dressed and lived simply, and never married. Although he was absorbed by his work and took on serious responsibilities, such as heading up all the artists of Herat, then of Persia, he felt apart from the world in which he lived. The trappings of success meant nothing to him. Many of his paintings show a beggar or other outcast, one who has the wisdom to join the elite and also the courage to eschew their eventual invitation. Discovering this, I heard clearly the voice of Anubis, the eternal outsider, partly in our world, partly in Bihzad's—but always alone.

Bihzad often put himself, or a representation of himself, into his paintings. Especially those paintings dealing with violence show a lone figure, apart from the fray, often behind a tree or boulder, watching the chaos below. It was Bihzad's way of showing his perplexity at the behaviors of most of the people in the world. Losing both of his parents at a young age would have also made him feel perpetually different from others. Primal loneliness can make us see ourselves as outside of the way regular people live. Bihzad seems to have spent almost all his life in the protected world of libraries, artists' colonies, and Sufi monasteries; yet his intelligence and sense of apartness led him to see into the world beyond that, where people had to struggle with loneliness and want.

At the time this story takes place, much of the world was engaged in the conflict that comes from growth. New ideas and experiences were smacking up against old beliefs, and there was no clear vision of which would take prominence. In Europe, the *Malleus Maleficarum* ("The Hammer of Witches"), a book justifying and encouraging the witch hunts, was published. The Cape of Storms (later called the Cape of Good Hope, at the southern edge of Africa) had just been rounded for the first time, establishing a new route to the Far East. Christopher Columbus was packing his bags to find a westerly route to the Indies. The Great Wall of China was being made even greater, new symbols for mathematical calculations were being invented, and Leonardo da Vinci was drawing in Milan. It was an exciting, if dangerous, time to be alive, as all of these developments were reflected in the art produced around the world.

Bihzad created tiny oasises of perfection, although he would not use that label. He painted small paintings, carefully balanced, restful to the eye even when disturbing to the mind. He took the art of miniature painting a great leap forward, and is justifiably known as one of the greatest Persian artists of all time.

A Time Line of Bihzad's Life

1460   Bihzad is born in Herat, in what is now Afghanistan. Persia is ruled by the Timurid Dynasty of Tamerlane. Herat is ruled by Sultan Husayn Mirza.

About 1468   Bihzad's parents die. Bihzad is brought up by Amir Ruhallah Mirak Hiravi, a renowned calligrapher and painter. Bihzad is raised in the library his guardian leads and is taught to paint.

About 1475   Bizhad studies under the esteemed painter of miniatures Mawlana Wali Allah.

1480   Mawlana Wali Allah dies.

Bihzad paints some of his earliest work, such as *A Poet Is Attacked by Dogs, Two Antelopes and Two Lynx,* and *A Youth Amongst Flowering Branches.*

Bihzad is initiated into the Naqshbandi order of Sufis.

1488   Bihzad paints *A Meeting of Scientists.*

1492   Jami dies.

1501   Mir Ali Shir, vizier to the sultan and patron of the arts, dies.

1507   Herat is captured by Shaybak Khan.
Bihzad becomes head of all artists in Herat.

1510   Shah Isma'il takes power in Herat, defeating Shaybek Khan.

1514   The shah hides Bihzad and other artists in a cave to prevent them from being captured by the Turks.
Prince Tahmasp becomes governor of Herat under Shah Isma'il.

About 1520 to 1528   Bihzad heads up a team of artists to create one of the greatest books ever produced in Iran, the nearly 800-page *Shah-namah.*

1522   Bihzad is appointed head of all artists in Persia.

1524   Shah Isma'il dies. Prince Tahmasp takes over.

1528   Bihzad moves to Tabriz to work with artists there.

1535   Bihzad dies.

1555   Mir Sayyid Ali, a student of Bihzad, goes to India to help found the Mughal school of painting.

For More Information

Bahari, Ebadollah. *Bihzad, Master of Persian Painting.* London: I. B. Tarus and Co. Ltd., 1996.

Baldock, John. *The Essence of Sufism.* London: Arcturus Publishing, 2004.

Hourani, Albert. *A History of the Arab Peoples.* Cambridge, Massachusetts: Belknap Press of Harvard University Press, 1991.

Shah, Indres. *The Way of the Sufi.* London: Jonathan Cape Ltd., 1968.

Stewart, Desmond. *Early Islam.* New York: Time-Life Books, 1967.